Man
from
Butte City

*Also by Lauran Paine
in Large Print:*

The Apache Kid
Cache Canon
The Devil on Horseback
The General Custer Story
Greed at Gold River
Lockwood
The Manhunter
The Misplaced Psyche
Murder Now Pay Later
Murder Without Motive
Tears of the Heart
Trail of the Freighters
The Triangle Murder
The White Bird

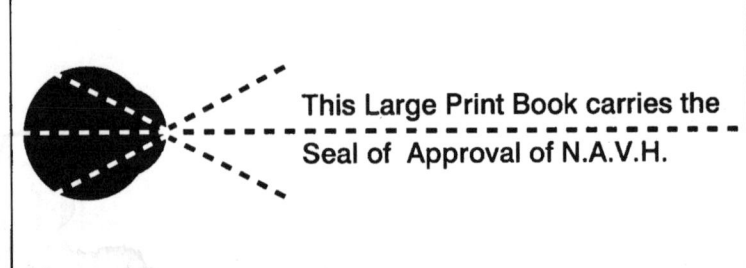
This Large Print Book carries the Seal of Approval of N.A.V.H.

Man from Butte City

LAURAN PAINE

G.K. Hall & Co. • Thorndike, Maine

Copyright © 1957 by Arcadia House

All rights reserved.

Published in 2000 by arrangement with Golden West Literary Agency.

G.K. Hall Large Print Paperback Series.

The text of this Large Print edition is unabridged.
Other aspects of the book may vary from the original edition.

Set in 16 pt. Plantin by Elena Picard.

Printed in the United States on permanent paper.

Library of Congress Cataloging-in-Publication Data

Paine, Lauran.
    Man from Butte City / by Lauran Paine.
      p. cm.
    ISBN 0-7838-8927-5 (lg. print : sc : alk. paper)
    1. Large type books.   I. Title.
PS3566.A34 M25 2000
    813'.54—dc21   99-089941

Man
from
Butte City

CHAPTER ONE

The land lay cowed under the lash of wind, and stinging dust tore at everything that dared stand against it. It was a land of distances so vast it ran interminably beyond the vision of the farthestseeing man or the perspective of the highest-flying buzzard. A land of contrasts, with immense buttes far to the north where the great swelling surge of country drifted off into obscurity; and closer, little gullies and serrated hillocks nestled side by side to pinch up against hogbacks where Indian trails as old as time itself wound.

The country was vast; it would take forever to tame it, and even then it would always harbor secret places. Nothing would ever change it, for there was no way to make it other than what it was.

Men lived there — not many — but some, and they knew instinctively that the only way a man could exist in that country was by adjusting to it. So they did what nature showed them they must do if they were to stay. They used it as the grazing range for wicked-horned, slab-sided, vicious, red-eyed cattle, as wild and tough and hard as the land itself. As hard as the men themselves, for everything that came and stayed in this land grew just as the country was — hard.

This hardness showed up in dozens of different ways in the people of the land. It depended on how their characters — their personalities — reacted to the imprint of the country's brand.

Some became silent and watchful, others became bitterly resentful.

And there would always be those who had an inherent capacity for evil. They would come into this land and look upon it with unseeing eyes, and smile at its limitless distances — and fail completely to grasp what was in the very air for thousands of untamed, unchanging, brooding miles.

Such a man rode down through the scourge of the desert wind with his shoulders humped against the fingers of dry cold that pummeled and kneaded him. His horse went along with his head hanging low, his eyes puckered and watering, and his mane and tail splayed and unkempt-looking, the electricity in the air making every hair stand out.

He rode down the wind-swirled wagon road toward the blistered, ugly clutch of buildings that seemed to merge with the timeless colors of the land itself. A village cast down in nowhere and left like that; leaning into itself for the only protection it could hope to find against the unleashed elements of the raw frontier.

In the wind there was a stifling sameness that gave an identical grey-beige tint to everything. And in the little town, with its warped wood and blistered paint, visible in the twin rows of buildings and the scattered houses around the village, that same strange hardness appeared; the one thing the fierce wind couldn't ever sweep away. It was part of the country and the people; part of the atmosphere.

But the man on the leggy black horse didn't feel it. For that matter, he never had felt kinship with anything outside himself; just a fanatical confidence in himself and the things he had applied himself to learn. These things were very useful in the places he went; deadly and terrible achievements.

He lifted his head once, just before he came into the town. The up-curl of his black hat, with its wide brim and dusty sweat stains on the headband showing through on the outside, was a graceful thing. So was the way he rode the black horse. So was the sense of easy power that was felt rather than seen. And so was the artistic sweep of the carved butt of his tied down, big blue gun, worn low on the right thigh.

He looked out at the town with a steady regard that showed nothing of the soul within that was impaled on spikes of ferocity. His glance was quick-moving but not restless; confident and poised in its own way, but unafraid and totally without emotion of any kind. It hadn't gotten like that naturally. There had been long years of training to make it that way. Years during which he'd come up out of a sordid environment and peeled away the things that hurt and pained a man. Years when an awful resentment blossomed into a contempt so supreme, so absolutely unquestioned by its possessor, that only two things remained where a conscience had once been — perfect coordination and perfect confidence. The only two things a topnotch gunfighter had to have and couldn't exist without.

He reined the gaunt black horse over into the perpetually open maw of a livery barn where the dust had sifted ankle-deep, and sat peering into the gloomy interior of the place. A faint aroma of ammonia and hay and manure came to him, but the wind snatched it and hurled it upward and away, and only the sad moaning sounds of the wind itself were left. That was when the man swung his head and looked up and down the single wide road of the town, then very tiredly swung his right leg around behind the cantle and came to rest on the ground beside his horse. He moved in out of the wind and stopped where there was a hushed vacuum, where neither man nor animal had to brace himself. It was when the tightness suddenly went out of them both that the lean, rangy frame wilted a little, and it was like that that the liveryman came out of his office and peered squintingly over at the stranger and saw him for the first time.

He was big but not heavy, tall but not outstandingly tall — and with an absolutely opaque blankness to his look that went with the rest of what the liveryman saw — and placed instantly. You didn't live all your life where death was closer than your elbow and not recognize it — almost smell it or sense it, and know a gunman when you saw one. Here was a killer like a machine — a conscienceless man whose entire existence revolved around just one thing — his gun. Death might come riding on a horse or stand hip-shot in the middle of the livery barn, waiting patiently and silently to give you the reins of his mount.

And the horse was always the best you'd seen in a long time, too. Those gunmen never had any assurance but what they saddled, so they always rode the best that money could buy. Such an animal was the leggy black, but right now he was tuckered out like a gutted snow-bird. He had come a long way but not fast, so the killer wasn't running. The liveryman thought all those things as he walked forward, hiding his real self behind a grin that was a mask. If the man wasn't running, then he was either riding through or staying. Staying meant killing.

"Howdy."

The black hat dipped a little and the blue eyes glanced at the first stall on the south side of the barn. It was a big, roomy box stall west of the combination office and harness room. "How much — stalled, grained and kept up?"

"Two bits a day."

The blue eyes came back and rested on the grinning face. "All right. Put him in that stall — that first one below the office there."

"Sure."

The reins changed hands and the gunman had

to stand a little straighter to plunge his left hand into a pants pocket and withdraw some money. He counted out big silver dollars and handed them over in an even amount and turned away, all in one motion. The liveryman had the answer to a question that had been nibbling at the far edges of his mind. No one riding through paid for more than a day; the stranger had paid for four weeks in advance. He was staying.

"What's the name of this place?"

The liveryman moved out of his reverie with a guilty feeling. He hadn't moved while watching the gunman's back as he went up toward the road. "Valverde."

The man's blue gaze held for a moment; then he turned and went out into the windstorm. The liveryman turned and led the gentle black horse after him. There was something to hope for if the stranger didn't know the town's name. But maybe not. Maybe he was just making sure.

The wind swooped down in a terrible gust that made the buildings of Valverde groan. It hoarded up the anguished sounds, gathered them unto itself, raised up with a shriek of abandon and flung itself out over the still, monotonous country that never changed.

In the wake of the big paroxysm, the gunman was crossing the dust-sprayed road when some residue left behind in the murky air cascaded down across him slantwise, under his jacket and down his neck. He just leaned farther forward into the backlash of the midget hurricane and kept on going. And that was a sign, too, for most of the men in that country would have cursed when the sharp stabbing stuff grated into their pores. The gunman didn't.

Diagonally, across from the livery barn was one of the two saloons of Valverde — The Drover's Rest. There was a card room in back, but for the most part men stayed out front around the small tables over against the wall on the north side of the big room. A bar ran from north to south, almost to the narrow opening to the card room and a little closet that was an office for Jorry Duncan, the owner. There was a stuffed head of a short-faced bear on one side of the backbar mirror and a mothy, huge, shaggy buffalo head on the south side of the glass.

The room had the boar's-nest odor of all purely masculine places. It wasn't caused just by liquor and tobacco and poor ventilation; it came from horse sweat and cow manure and man sweat too, all blended into a smell that wasn't actually unpleasant, strangely enough.

The day barman was one of those misfits who was imprisoned in his job because of a physical defect that kept him grounded in this country where every able-bodied man made his living from the back of a horse. It hadn't been altogether an accident when Frank Leslie — "Buckskin" Frank Leslie, part myth, part legend, part Satyr — had ridden through and fought Mort Emmons over a dance hall girl; a fight that left

Mort behind in Valverde with a knee so thoroughly torn apart and ruined that his leg was as stiff as his conviction was strong that no woman alive was worth that much.

Oddly, Mort, the unhorsed horseman, wasn't bitter and resentful and disagreeable. It wasn't his nature to brood, and if it had been he wouldn't have done it, because he'd found that bartending gave a man no longer fired with the false, lurid impulses of youth a fascinating insight into his fellow creatures. Mort had learned long ago — before the grey had come sparingly, surreptitiously, into his magnificent moustache and shock of coarse, thick hair — that the side people perpetually showed to the world wasn't actually what they were like underneath at all.

He was a student of men of long standing, so when the gunman shouldered into the room out of the wind, Mort looked straight at him and let all the emanations that came out of him filter across the roiled dust of the atmosphere and form a hard ball in which Mort read his character. The man was a killer. You didn't need experience to see that. But here was one of the strangest killers Mort had ever seen — or sensed, rather — because he brought out of the storm with him only a blank impassivity; nothing more. There was nothing alarming or venomous or hating, nothing vicious or especially deadly in the man, and that was what impressed Mort most. The nothingness; the absolute wall of blankness. Mort was vastly interested right away, partly because the day was a total waste as far as the bar was concerned — he got a percentage from Jorry Duncan — and partly because he couldn't recall ever having had the same feeling of uncertainty or mystification about a man before.

The stranger crossed to the bar, lowered his head, opened his jacket, pulled out his shirt-tail and shook himself like a dog coming out of a creek. Just as methodically he stuffed in the shirt again and buttoned up the jacket, lifted his vacant blue eyes and looked straight into Mort's eyes. "Dust," he said, and his voice was as colorless as the rest of him. The strangest man Mort Emmons had ever run across, and he'd known a few in his time. He nodded his head understandingly.

"Ale?"

The blue eyes drifted casually from the bear head to the buffalo head and back to Mort's face, all in one liquid, fluid movement that took in everything. "Sour mash."

Mort served him and turned his back. He knew when they wanted to talk and when they didn't. This one didn't; in fact, Mort would have bet a sound horse he didn't talk anyway, unless he had something to say. Curiosity made Mort sneak little stabbing glances at the gunman's face by way of the backbar mirror. It wasn't an especially hard face and certainly not a drunken face as most gunmen's faces were — and that was bad. This kind was the most deadly of all.

They never over-drank, never over-talked. They were like ice inside and out; better yet, like one of those upland lakes back over where the Indians still hung out. Still-moving; deeper than anyone knew. Absolutely merciless, but handsome. He *was* handsome, too. His eyes were well set beneath a forehead that ran under the upcurve of his big black hat, and his cheeks were ruddy, lean and smooth. His nose was a trifle hawkish — hooked just a little, but not much — and thin, so that the nostrils flared outward; and his mouth was pressed flat from long habit and an inner strength — or fierceness. He was long and thin-lipped but not harsh or cruel-looking. The biggest paradox to Mort, though, was the way he stood and carried himself. He was not stooped or careless or loose-muscled, but erect with a swinging grace. Goldarnedest killer Mort Emmons had ever seen. He looked like a successful cowman or a very confident lawman or something else respectable — and yet there was that killer look to him that was unmistakable.

"You get much wind like this around here?"

Mort faced back with a hitch of his trousers. "Naw, not a lot — maybe three, four days a year. This is the worst I seen it in six years. It's a heller all right." He considered. He'd like to know if the gunman had been riding in it — and more. But no — the question had really invited nothing more than he'd already said. He reached down under the backbar and fished a shot glass out of the brackish water in the wash-bucket and killed time swabbing it out with the sour rag draped from his belt.

The gunman wasn't even looking at him. He was standing a little sideways, looking back out into the storm and beyond, to the dim, dust-mottled silhouettes that were buildings across the road. "Raise a lot of cattle hereabouts?"

"Quite a few. There's some purty big ranches in this country."

"Yeah?"

"Yeah. There's three big ones. Altogether they run about twelve thousand head in these hills. Biggest's the Crownover outfit. Owned by Ashley Crownover — Old Ash, the boys call him. He runs over three thousand head."

The gunman didn't seem to be listening any more, and Mort let silence come back and settle between them. After a while, when the sour mash was gone, the gunman turned fully and leaned on the counter. Before, he'd stood beside it, relaxed and aloof. Now he looked steadily into Mort's face. "You know a feller named Duncan here in Valverde?"

The question startled Mort but he didn't show it. The gunman didn't see the quick fluttering of his hands as he twisted the damp rag stuck in his belt. His mind was working when he answered, too. "Yeah. He owns this saloon."

Mort had no especial liking for Jorry Duncan; few people had for that matter. He was a cold, calculating man who had an enormous capacity for planning ahead and creating facts out of little things he heard and was told. A man whose brilliance of mind wasn't matched by any kind of standards or ethics that Mort had ever been able to discover. A wispy individual within a strange, devious world of his own creating. Merciless and vastly superior in mental ability to most of the men of this land, but absolutely lacking in any of their crude decencies. Had Jorry sent for a killer? Why did this gunman — who resembled Jorry in some ways but differed in others — want him? Jorry had the best business in Valverde. Mort knew that this wouldn't ever keep a man like Duncan from wanting other things. But why would Jorry get mixed up with a killer like this? It didn't make sense — but it did make a ripple of fear stir in the depths of a man.

"You want to see him?"

"Yeah. Where is he?"

Mort jerked his head. "Around the end of the bar by the buffler head. That little doorway there on your left. That's his office. Came in a couple of hours ago."

The blue eyes never wavered. "You go tell him there's a man out here wants to see him. All right?"

"Sure."

Mort went, worried and perplexed enough not to realize he'd been ordered to do something he wouldn't normally have done. Normally, he'd have smiled thinly and jerked his head for the gunman to go himself. This was different. Anything that materially affected Jorry Duncan also affected Mort Emmons. He had his percentage in The Drover's Rest to think of.

Duncan's voice answered the knock and Mort went into the little room. There wasn't anything in it but a scuffed roll-top desk backed against the wall, an equally abused captain's chair with wire twisted around the legs to keep them from wavering, and a squat, massive little safe with an improbably fat angel painted on it in ivory with a green cloud for a background. One other chair was back in the far corner, as though reluctantly put in the room.

Jorry Duncan's build was slight; he was small-boned and finely made. His hands were long and white, like his face, but the receding hairline added an incongruous look of nobility to the even, too perfect features that was belied by the hands. Jorry's eyes were large and wet-looking, almost limpid. They contrasted in their gentleness to the bloodless, lipless line that was his narrow mouth above a slightly pointed chin. He wore a look he had cultivated so well over the years that it always lurked just behind any facial expression he had — even anger; a look of pleasant inquisitiveness, harmless and diffident and false. Mort Emmons knew the look very well. It was a classical example of a person showing an exterior that wasn't really his at all.

"Jorry — there's a man outside wants you to come out an' see him."

Duncan's smile held. The inquisitiveness was

more marked, though. "If he wants me, Mort — send him back here."

"He won't come."

Jorry's expression looked a little strained, annoyed rather than curious. "He won't? Did you ask him?"

"No."

"How do you know he won't then, Mort?"

"Because he told me to fetch you out there."

Jorry laughed with a little squirting sound. "Who the devil does he think he is? I don't run up to meet everybody who wants to see me. Tell him . . ."

"Tell him yourself," Mort said, irritated beyond reason. "He's a gunman."

Jorry's smile faded so gradually it was hardly noticeable, but his eyes didn't move at all. They bored into Mort Emmons for a second before he pushed softly away from the desk and stood up. "All right," he said. "I'll go out."

In the wake of Mort's stiff-legged gait, Jorry stopped in the narrow opening and looked quickly along the bar where a steady pair of blue eyes were watching him. He made his face curl into an inquisitive little smile and walked forward right up to where the lean man was waiting. Jorry nodded toward the tables up against the north wall and went on over. For just a second, Mort, who was watching them, didn't think the gunman was going to concede to the suggestion, but he did, walking with a rolling-hipped gait. Light on his feet, Mort thought. Light and quick, like a cougar — and just about as friendly. Jorry sat down and motioned toward the opposite chair. The gunman remained standing, but he fished out a tobacco sack and worked up a cigarette as he stood there.

"You wanted to see me?"

The blue eyes flicked ironically over Jorry's face and went back to the cigarette as though it were far more important. "I'm Bent Sutton. You sent for me."

"Oh." Jorry flashed a nervous glance back over at Mort. The bartender couldn't hear what they said. The distance was too great. Moreover, they didn't want him to. The bartender was busy; at least he wasn't looking their way. Jorry shot his glance back to the gunman. He was smoking now, standing there and looking down at Jorry like an Indian. Irritated because the gunman was above him, forcing him to look up, and because he was obviously not a man who met other men on anything less than an equal status, Jorry frowned. It emphasized the pinched narrowness above the bridge of his nose and made him look mean and cold. "Sit down."

The gunman's appraisal of Jorry Duncan wasn't flattering. That was instantly apparent. "I'll stand," he said. "Let's get this over with. Who is he and how do I get to him?"

The palms of Jorry's hands grew damp with a greasy oiliness. Here was death waiting to be directed. This was a lot different from just planning what he had in mind. And Mort — he was no fool. Jorry wasn't a cursing man, but he swore under his breath anyway. He looked up in quick outrage at the peaceful, still face of the killer. "Come on in the office."

"Never mind that. I haven't got the time." The blue eyes were opaque. "Spit it out and give me the money and let's get it over with."

"It isn't that easy."

The gunman's face settled into a very faint but unmistakable expression of impatience. Smoke drifted out around the cigarette when he spoke, and the words were made thick and unnatural by it. "Duncan — I didn't come down here because I wanted to. You sent word along the back-trail. I got it. Here I am. Now cough up the name, the place, and the money, and let's get it over with. I don't like your country." He seemed on the verge of saying more, but he didn't.

Jorry's hands were not the only part of him that was damp now. He hated this gunman with a loathing based on fear. He looked out at the wild wind and the noontime glimmer where a pallid sun was trying to hold its own against impossible odds.

"His name's Ashley Crownover. He's got a ranch not over seven miles northwest of town. He'll ride into town today because I sent for him. He'll use the old road that branches off the main trace about six miles north of here. He'll be along that road —" Jorry turned and shot a worried look at the clock over the backbar, up high, where it was reasonably safe — "in another two hours. Supposed to meet me here at three o'clock."

"I'm to get him on the road. That right?"

"Yes."

"Will he be alone?"

"I don't know."

The gunman shrugged slightly, still smoking. "Doesn't make much difference," he said. "All right; where's the money?"

"In my office."

"Good. Go get it."

Jorry did, avoiding Mort's quick glance, moving fast as though he had just seen something he wanted to get away from. When he returned it was with high color under his pale skin so that his moist-looking eyes shone out of an unnaturally ruddy face. Mort saw the expression, although Jorry avoided him again. Jorry was nervous. He always got red and sweaty-looking like that when he was shaken up. Now, though, it was worse than usual because even his eyes were shiny.

Jorry's back was to the bartender when he stopped before the gunman and held something out. The gunman looked down, squinting against the upthrust of eye-stinging smoke. He counted something and fisted it. Shoving it into his pants pocket, he had to haul up straighter. The old levis were tight.

"All right, Duncan, you can quit worrying."

But Jorry couldn't. He was just beginning to worry. "Are you coming back to Valverde?"

A cold grunt. "No, what for? You got another one?"

"No. . . . Just Crownover. I was wondering is all."

"Nope. You'll never see me again unless you send up word. I'll move out as soon's it's over. I come in, get the job done and move out. It's the best way." He was turning, brushing past Jorry, as he said the last sentence; he headed toward the door and the howling frightfulness outside. Jorry watched him go and felt that he had never met a man like Bent Sutton before. A human piece of ice. A functioning, animated, lean hunk of flesh and blood destructiveness. He didn't turn and look at Mort for fully five minutes. It took him that long to get back enough control to lever up the inquisitive smile and make it into a mask again. By then Bent Sutton was bucking the wind-drifts toward the livery barn while Valverde huddled indoors. His passing was unmarked by all but Jorry Duncan, Mort Emmons, and the liveryman who saw him looking up out of the fierce wind and dust. The hostler wore a wondering look. Anyone who'd ride out in such weather was crazy.

"Your horse?"

"No, one of your livery horses. The best one you've got. Put my saddle on him and hurry up."

The hostler hurried for two reasons. The gunman was one reason, of course, but the coal-oil stove going in the office was his other reason. It was getting cold now. Early spring, high wind, a gunman, and a cold snap to boot. God A'mighty — what a day!

Bent Sutton eyed the horse. It was as good as he'd expected. He glanced overhead at the clock cased in ancient streamers of flypaper, dropped his glance to the liveryman, turned and swung up. The wind wailed and beat with tiny fists all over the old building. He rode out into it, swung north and roweled the livery animal once, to show who was up there on his back. After that the beast went obediently, if not willingly, into the sideslip of the windstorm.

Bent's head was tucked low and his jacket pulled in and made fast around him. And he was grinning. Nature was good when you understood her. In a windstorm, for example, you could ride right into a town and shoot a man and ride out again. There were no tracks to be followed. For a thousand dollars a man could stand a little wind, a little discomfort, even talking to men like Jorry Duncan.

He thought of Duncan and the impassiveness returned. It hadn't always been Jorry Duncan. Time had a way of being good to people sometimes, whether they deserved it or not. If they lasted long enough, they'd get a favor from fate some day.

The horse went along with his eyes almost closed. He blew his nose often and tilted his head a little to the left so the wind and dust wouldn't blow into his ear. It made an uneasy sound, and tickled.

There was a fork-off where the beast seemed to hesitate. Bent leaned forward and studied it, holding the reins high against his chest with his left hand. The distance was about right and it looked like a ranch road. He reined over and squeezed the livery animal with his legs. It went willingly, as though it had been over this trail before and knew there was a flake of hay at the other end.

Bent rode with his eyes almost closed against the force of wind. He could peer through the black lashes and get a sort of hazy idea of the lay of the country ahead. It was a jumble where the road dipped and flung itself up out of gullies and went limping along over sidehills, then straight as a die up an ancient creekbed that had been dry since the year one. That was what he'd been looking for: a place where there were slopes and brush and even junipers and jack-pines; a place with available concealment handy.

He stopped again and gauged the distance from the road to a little plateau. You always stayed well within accurate shooting distance. One shot — even if you missed — never gave your position away. Two shots did. If you didn't get your victim, he could guess about where you were, and that wasn't any good, because you didn't want to be pinned down in a silly, drawn-out gunfight.

Bent goaded the livery horse up the little incline against the beast's better judgment. He got him all the way to the top and stepped off. Untying one of the split-reins, he made a fetlock-hobble of the line, then waved the horse away where he wouldn't show against the murky skyline. After that there was plenty of time to go over everything again. Squatting just over the lip of the plateau near a sour-smelling little old juniper that was being shriven and tortured by the gale, he estimated the distance to the roadbed, sighted with his pistol, holding it like a man who had been raised with one in his hand; lightly, confidently, easily, professionally.

The distance was right. The weather was perfect. No sign would be left behind, there would be no glimpse of the assassin until it was too late, and the howling wilderness that increased as the afternoon wore on would gobble up the thunderous echo and muzzle blast.

He didn't smile but he could have. Rarely before had he had everything just right. There was the discomfort, but that wasn't anything. Not to a man who'd lived the way Bent Sutton had. He settled down on the lee side of the threshing, straining juniper and waited. That was all that was left to do — wait.

While he sat hunched up under the meager protection of the old tree, his body might have been content to remain inert but his mind wasn't. The longer the passage of time the further back his memory went, until it was in a town something like Valverde, only dirtier and closer to the border. There was a big-eyed, skinny kid with smarting places under his rags to remind him of the drunken mother in the shack with its stench and flies and its clutter of whiskey bottles. There was little pleasant to remember until the time he'd found the lost colt and had taken it back into the bottoms of the willow-creek bed and made it a secret corral where he could rub noses with it and smell its clean animal fragrance. They were two animals needing something neither understood, and getting it from each other.

Then one day three men had come, puffing and cursing and fighting their way through the stiff-whipping willows, tracking him to the little corral. They stood there with moving eyes and still faces, looking down at him where he knelt by the little jag of stolen hay he'd so laboriously carried in, armful by armful, against the encroaching winter, for his colt.

Two of them had been brutal enough, but the third hadn't said much. In fact that last one, the oldest man, had finally sworn at the other two when they slammed him down against the earth as he jumped up in quavering fright and tried to run. Bent remembered his words very clearly. The man had said, "That's enough of that, you two. Let him up an' keep your hands to yourselves."

Then he remembered the long, sideling look of the rancher he'd stolen the hay from. The man didn't say much — not to Bent anyway. Just gave him a long sly look and a brittle little laugh. "All right, let him go. I'll get paid."

Bent lost the colt. His mother beat him and

threw two bottles at him, but her aim was never any good. But she knew about the colt, and sold him to some Mexicans and bought fresh whiskey and got so drunk he didn't get anything to eat for two days. That was when he'd left and gone wandering like a coyote, living where he could, developing a coyote's awareness and courage, his shiftiness and bitterness, until he'd grown up, inside, away ahead of his years, and come to hate people because they had cuffed him and run him off.

And out of that crucible of hatred had come a gunman. It hadn't been a quick evolution, though. Bent Sutton was a boy before he was a man. He ran with those who would tolerate him and learned from them. His life was made up of evil, and he achieved a prominence as a badman because he knew no trade. He had no earlier standards to overcome, and grew to manhood with a string of crimes so long he himself couldn't begin to remember them all. But this was the first time he'd ever hired out his gun for a clear-cut, out-and-out, bushwhacking murder. Not that he wouldn't have done it before; he'd just never been hired to do it. The stages and trains robbed, the cattle whisked away in the night, the horses stolen in a wild run that defied capture, and the holdups — these were endless, it seemed, until now he stood as high as a man could get in his profession.

One thousand dollars for killing one man. One thousand dollars an hour. Bent Sutton was among the foremost outlaws of his era, and he knew it with a cold sense of achievement. There wasn't a man anywhere on earth who would meet him as anything less than an equal. That was the reward for fighting back at life. If a man lived long enough, Bent had often thought — as he had about Jorry Duncan back in the town of Valverde — time would favor him. All he had to do was train himself for the day so he would be ready.

He hugged in closer to the tree and rubbed one arm with one hand — his gun hand. It was cold all of a sudden, and the wind wasn't ever going to let up. What an untamed giant of a country. Big — bigger than anything he'd ever seen before — wild as it would always be, and hard. But Bent Sutton was harder. He'd whisk in, earn his thousand, and ride out again. And there was one other thing he planned on doing, for Jorry Duncan had no edge on deceit. Bent knew his way around too. That was why he'd paid up in advance for the black horse's keep.

Finally he smiled. Jorry Duncan. Duncan nothing! Maybe the so-called Jorry Duncan didn't remember, but a skinny kid grown to a lean, tall man *did* remember. A horse whinnied somewhere behind him. With a swirling curse he swung around against the tree. The livery animal had heard or scented another animal. Crownover must not have kept to the road. It all flashed through his mind like a sharp, stabbing warning of peril.

He stood up and let the gun hang at his side, inwardly sweating. A man didn't make mistakes like this. Not when he had a gun in his hand. That was part of what he'd schooled himself to think ahead to, because an outlaw gambling with his only life never got a second chance.

The wind was carrying everlasting sharp particles of dust into his face. He squinted into it, his nostrils pinched against the pent up expulsion of breath. He could see the livery horse. He could also see another horse standing beside it with a rider up. And he could see the rider peering at him through the murk.

He holstered the gun carefully, turning a little as he did so. He stepped up onto the plateau's rim and walked very slowly toward the horseman — and got a shock. It wasn't a horseman. . . . It was a girl. A girl with a cold face, perfect features, and a blue bandana tied around her hair under a tugged-down hat brim.

She looked at him strangely; he couldn't shake off his uneasiness so fast. Some of it was mirrored in his eyes, whether he knew or cared or not. If she hadn't been a girl — if she'd been a lawman with a gun or a cowman named Crownover with a suspicion —

He got close enough to see her lips moving and caught some of what she said.

"Not lost, are you?"

CHAPTER TWO

She had her face turned toward him, away from the wild wind, and her eyes were open and intent-looking. His face, turned toward the gale, was shuttered tightly, and his eyes were nearly hidden behind his black lashes as he studied her. He didn't answer right away. He never spoke until he was ready to.

She was poised and perfect, well-formed and sturdy, with a look of confidence that he liked. Not many girls coming upon a strange man in a windstorm would have been so detached and calm.

"No, I'm not lost. Are you?"

"No, I live out here."

The way she said it, it sounded as though she were an integral part of this angry, huge country. He looked down at the horse's left shoulder, where the shaggy winter hair was slipping and a deeper blending of color made a design. A crown over a single bar. That would be Crownover's brand. This was either a Crownover or someone who lived on the Crownover ranch. He looked up at her again and found the greenish-blue of her eyes still on him with open and frank curiosity.

"You a Crownover?"

"Yes. Antonia Crownover. Who are you?"

That shook him. Common frontier etiquette deplored blunt questions like that. At least in his world. She wouldn't know that, though — or would she? Rich people were sometimes rude in a studied way. He let his squinted-up glance ramble over her features, but there was nothing there to indicate how she'd meant it. Her mouth was full and rich-looking and stung a rosy color by the particles of stone-dust in the wind. He didn't answer at all because he wasn't sure how he should answer.

Well, if Ashley Crownover was coming along behind his daughter somewhere, or if he'd sent her on ahead, or if she had just been out riding — it didn't make any difference. You couldn't cut a man down in cold blood with a witness around. He turned slowly, went around the head of her horse, stooped and yanked the rein hobble off his livery animal. Without looking over at her, he swiped at the dusty seat leather, swung up and gigged the beast.

He didn't turn to look back either, but rode all the way back to Valverde with his head sunk on his chest again and the annoying dust filtering down his neck and working into his flesh like mica.

At the livery barn he stepped down without a word, turned and struck out across the roadway toward The Drover's Rest. Not until he was inside did irritation come to him, and that was prompted as much by the sticky, itching sensation under his clothes as by the happenstance that had come so awkwardly, blunderingly, to spoil what should have been as good an ambushing expedition as a man had ever hoped for. The lousy wind hadn't been altogether on his side or it wouldn't have let that girl ride up over the plateau instead of sticking to the road as she should have.

That girl —

"Bran mash?"

Bent looked up from the repeated chore of shaking out as much of the fine dust as he could and stuffing in his shirt tail. The bartender's face was cold and inscrutable-looking. He nodded. "Yeah."

Over the drink that let new warmth and the slightest of sullen fires course under his hide, he thought of her. What the devil had she been doing up there, anyway? You didn't ride a rim when the wind was blowing; you stayed down in the valley where that ranch road was. Pretty. Hard to say what there was in a woman that attracted a man. In some, it was the features; in others, the poise; in others, both. As for Bent Sutton — he didn't know.

He'd known women when he'd wanted to, on both sides of the line. They were a convenience, like drinking water when he passed a spring in the desert, but there was no place in his world for them and his own world was all he cared about. He was the disciple of his own laws, his own hungers and his own philosophy of scorn. It wasn't hate as it had been once. Not now — when he was coming into the prime — the very peak of his life. He could afford scorn now, so he used it in the place of the resentment-inspired jealousy that had always been hatred before. But that girl up there in the wild wind —

"Another one?"

It startled him. He looked into the glacial face with its strong, craggy boniness behind the handsome greying moustache that dropped a little, then flared up into buffalo-horn curls. He ignored the barman's question and posed one of his own. "You know most of the folks around here?"

"Enough of them," Mort said.

The gunman looked down at his empty, sticky glass. "Would you give a man an idea about one — if he asked it?"

After a second's hesitation, Mort nodded. A name would tell him a lot right now, and he was as curious as the devil. Especially since Jorry and this hombre had talked. "I reckon. Who?"

"Crownover."

Mort eased his weight onto his good leg and stood back so he could lean on the backbar shelves. "Well, Old Ash came into the country about thirty years ago, they say. They also say he came in a heck of a hurry, but I don't know about that. I do know he's rich and plenty tough. I rode for the outfit for three years."

"He got a wife?"

"Nope. She died four, five years back. I knew her real well. She used to come down to the corrals and watch me rein horses. Was a real lady."

"Mexican?"

Mort's eyes dropped quickly to the gunman's face. "Why'd you say that?"

The blank blue eyes matched the shrug the gunman gave. "Just a guess. Was she?"

"Naw; maybe half."

But Mort wasn't stupid. Antonia Crownover. This killer knew her. Watching for a reaction, he said, "There's a daughter. We used to call her 'Tonia — or just Tonie — when she was little."

The gunman's face told Mort nothing, but he spoke in a way that made Mort aware of his way of thinking. "Yeah, she looks about eighteen."

"No, she'd have to be closer to twenty-two."

The gunman's eyes had adopted that peculiar withdrawn expression Mort had seen before. He wouldn't go any farther with the conversation. It was closed from now until he brought it up again. But Mort didn't care. He had plenty of room for thought. Crownover. Jorry wasn't going after *that* now, was he?

As though prompted out of his seclusion by Mort's thoughts, Jorry Duncan strolled into the barroom — and stopped. The gunman was looking over at him and Jorry's stare wasn't nearly as contained as Bent Sutton's was. Mort watched with a sinking sensation because Jorry's face was a dead giveaway. It was the Crownover outfit Jorry was after — the runty little buzzard — and the gunman was his tool.

Bent felt disgust seep into his face and for once

made no effort to conceal his feelings. He turned and walked over to one of the north-wall tables and sat down. Instantly Jorry followed him. He didn't sit until Bent inclined his head.

"I didn't get him."

Jorry's eyes held to the hawkish features. "What happened?"

The disgust grew. "Don't worry; I will. Just couldn't do it today. A girl rode up behind me before I even saw the feller."

"His daughter," Jorry said, letting his eyes slip unseeingly off Sutton's face. "Antonia."

Bent said nothing for a while. "You got rooms upstairs?"

"Yeah."

"Fetch me a key. I'll hang over here for a day or two until I do your job for you."

Jorry got the key from behind the bar off a smooth board with nails in it. More keys were hanging there. Bent took it in his palm and got up without looking at Jorry Duncan again. He shot Mort Emmons a quick glance. "You got a roustabout?"

"Somewhere," Mort said, reluctantly pleased that the killer showed him more regard than Jorry, "but I haven't seen him today. You want water toted?"

"Yeah. Hunt him up and send him around."

Up under the roof of the saloon, the wind sounded like a handmaiden of destruction every time it whooped into the pitch and went slanting over, striking with terrifying force all along the shingles until it got to the ridgepole and went free again. The room was chilly but not awfully cold, and Bent sought out the tub room and saw that someone was already hauling water for his bath.

He bathed, paid the perspiring Mexican who had hauled up the buckets, re-dressed, after shaking and beating his clothes free of the worst of the dust, then sat down and very methodically began cleaning his gun and thinking.

He had known who Jorry Duncan was when he'd gotten the word that he wanted a killing done. Where Duncan was concerned, he had a deep-rankling sense of injustice that his last trip to the town of his birth had made vengefully important to him. Let Jorry think he was going to ride away after killing Crownover.

Jorry was brilliant and sly and steeped in evil. But he didn't know something his hired killer knew. Bent looked up from cleaning his gun, wiped his hands and made a cigarette and smiled at the wall. Killing Duncan would be the easiest thing on earth. A man such as he was died easily. Their forte was deceit and superior brain power, not gunpowder. A better way to beat him would be to outsmart him. Jorry Duncan loved money. That was how to beat him — with fear and refined robbery. Bent went back to cleaning the gun, a cruel smile lingering around his eyes, and the cigarette smoke working, worrying its way up over his handsome face and past the burnished copper of his hair, adding to the draughty mustiness of the little room.

When he slept, later, it was with a sense of satisfaction such as he'd never felt before, and he felt the same way when he awoke, went downstairs, ate a solid breakfast, got his black horse and went for a ride over a cowed and still countryside. The wind had fled during the night but signs of its passage were everywhere. In crannies it was six inches thick, and the ruts of the roadway north out of Valverde were sifted over so that his horse sank inches deep into the spongy grains of the milleniums.

Bent saw the immensity of the country and felt the brooding agelessness as he rode northward, far past the cut-off he'd taken the day before. He cut inland to the west and made a casual sweep of the range beyond.

Once, on a hogback, he got a good picture of the land. It wasn't clear yet, with the dust still hovering over the distances, but he saw enough. Off to his left was a big valley with a snake-like ditch that stole away the residue overflow from a mountain creek and carried the water overhead, to a big, uneven patch of green where some massive buildings were. That would be Crownover's ranch. He could see where the ranch road came worming through a plum thicket, past a cottonwood grove, and up to the yard where corrals and barns and bunkhouses and the main log house stood.

The bartender had said that Crownover's

outfit was big. Bent got off his horse, squatted and knuckled back his black hat. It was big all right — darned big. The kind of a ranch to fit the size of the country. A man could squat up above it and study things for hours and get them all worked out in his mind.

"Lookin' for something?"

Instinctive anger flooded through Bent. For the second time in two days someone had come up behind him. He got up slowly and turned. Two riders were sitting there staring stonily at him. One was thin and cadaverous-looking, with a muddy complexion, like a man bothered by a bad kidney. The other man was almost square. Not tall yet not short, he was massive and wore a little van dyke beard that accentuated the darkness of his eyes, glued now to Bent's face with an arrogant challenge.

"Just looking," Bent said, still feeling anger at himself for being caught off-guard again. "You mind?"

The thin rider said nothing. If anything, he looked a little embarrassed, as though he knew the man he was with well enough to realize there would be some nastiness shown whether it was called for or not.

The blocky rider's glance held like black iron. "Where you from?"

"Different places," Bent said, finding a ready outlet for his inverted wrath and transferring it to the bearded man along with a quick and instinctive dislike. "Where *you* from?"

For a second the thick-thewed man didn't answer; then he lifted his right hand from behind the swells of his saddle, and Bent saw the solitary black eye of a gunbarrel peering at him. The man's face didn't change an iota. He spoke in an aside to the skinny cowboy. "Take your rope and snare him, Dave."

Bent was astonished more than anything else. He made no move to side-step the little bear-cat loop that raised, dropped, and was jerked snug around his ankles. Questions jumped into his mind but he asked none of them. He didn't get the chance, because Van Dyke was speaking again.

"We don't like sneaks spying on the ranch, mister. We don't like strangers around here a-tall. Remember that." The swift, sharp cocking of his hand gun was even more eloquent than the words. No man had gotten the drop on Bent Sutton in over four years. That smarted worse than the improbable thing that was happening. Van Dyke reined his horse out of the way, back to one side, and held the cocked gun so that its spout was full on Bent's belly; then he spoke to the skinny rider.

"Ride off, Dave."

Dave did. The rest of what happened was a kaleidoscope of pain and dimly remembered bumping. Once, at first, Bent had rolled over and used his palms to shield his face, but not for long. They wore through to the pads of flesh and failed him. Shortly after that his head, lolling drunkenly, had collided with a lichen rock which knocked him senseless. That was when the black-eyed man had called out, " 'Nuff, Dave. He can't feel it no more."

Sensibility was a long time returning. The sun was setting when Bent looked up, but didn't move. His body was afire with scratches and bruises. He lay there thinking it was lucky for him he could still see. Then memory came back clearly and he rolled over, grunted annoyance at the pain, got up and looked at himself. His levis, old anyway, were in rags. His shirt was stiff with shed blood, and filthy. His hands — he did swear then — he tried to work the swollen fingers that wouldn't close but halfway. . . .

He got back atop the black horse, stirred him out of his drowsiness with spurs which were blunted and stone-scratched, and rode back toward Valverde. He timed it so that his arrival was after dark. He hunted up the local doctor and lied in the same unemotional voice he always used.

"Got hung up in the stirrup and dragged."

The doctor said very little and worked with an annoyed frown. It was tedious and uninteresting work to be dragged away from supper for. When he was finished, he eyed the lean, hard-looking rider with something akin to dislike and said: "Five dollars."

Bent sensed his attitude, fished out ten dollars and passed them over. Scornfully, he said, "Oh, it's worth more'n that, Doc. Buy yourself a new pick with the difference — get a sharp one next time." Then he went out into the night, led his horse around to the back of the livery barn, handed over the reins in the dark and walked across the littered lot next to the barn, through the deepest shadows to the rickety stairs.

In his room, he waited with the patience of an Indian until he heard the roustabout packing water for someone's bath; then he nailed him and poked another ten dollars out through the crack in the door, along with his tattered clothing. "Here; go buy me another pair of pants and another shirt and keep the change. Make it fast. And fetch back some goose-grease salve."

He made a lumpy cigarette and waited. It didn't take long. The Mexican had been inspired by the money left over. Bent took the package through the crack of the door, ordered another bath, then looked over his new levis and butter-nut-colored shirt.

It was late by the time he got the bath, and later still before he fell asleep. But when he awoke his body ached rather than burned, and that was something he wasn't used to. Still, he stayed put for three full days, letting the roustabout make money off him for meals and more baths until he was pretty well back to normal. When he went down into The Drover's Rest, Mort Emmons eyed him with surprise. Nothing spectacular had happened since the gunman had shown up in Valverde. . . .

"Bran mash?"

"Yeah." He waited until the crowd thinned out a little, then took his drink down around the bend in the bar and looked at the men very carefully. Van Dyke wasn't there, nor was the skinny man called Dave. He caught Mort's eye. The bartender went down and leaned against the wall, sticking his stiff leg out in front of him.

"You know a heavy built feller with a little van dyke chin beard? A sort of bossy-acting cuss?"

Mort swung his eyes to the lean face. "That'd be Crownover's foreman."

"Oh? What's his name?"

"Holt. I don't know his front name. The boys call him Van, 'cause of his beard. What about him?" Mort felt there was a certain intimacy between them now that would allow him to risk a question. He saw an instant chill come into the gunman's face and linger for a moment, before it went away and words came.

"Sort of a disagreeable cuss, isn't he?"

"I reckon," Mort said guardedly. The fact that he had no use whatsoever for Holt didn't cause him to lose his caution. Mort disliked Ashley Crownover almost as much as he disliked his foreman, but in a different way.

"Has that Crownover outfit been having trouble lately?"

"Not that I know of. They're pretty set in their ways though." Mort had seen the scabbed hands minutes before. He needed no second look to confirm his suspicion. "You run afoul of Van?"

"Yeah."

"Well," Mort said, "one thing a feller wants to watch on Crownover range — don't be there unless you got a darned good reason. That's Old Ashley's way of making sure no one moves off with any of his stock. It's a long-standing rule. They had it when I worked there, too. Good business. They don't lose nearly as much stuff as other outfits around here. Remember — between the hold-out Injuns in the back country and the Border — they got to be pretty hard."

"Yeah." There was a little pause; then: "Thanks."

Mort nodded. He had only one more fleeting glance at the gunman; then someone was pounding the bar up at the far end — over by the short-faced bear's head — calling his name.

Bent finished his drink and went across to the livery barn. This time he saddled up by himself and strapped the rifle-boot under his right rosadero, with the carbine butt forward and slanting back almost level with his saddle-fork. He rode out into the spring slash of sunlight directly overhead, swung north and kicked the leggy black out into a long-legged, easy lope. The shambling indifference of his former ride out of town was gone now. Bent Sutton had a destination and a goal.

He circled over the Crownover range and stayed off the skyline, like an Indian. No outlaw or Indian ever rode atop a hill. They rode just below the ridge so that they were partly camouflaged by the drabness of the country, but they rode so they could see all around too. Bent rode like that now. The sun was slanting off-center a little, and shadows that all day long had been huddling beneath rocks and trees slipped out silently and poked little fingers into the places where the sun had been.

He rode constantly, not stopping once, searching for other riders until he found them. Then, to his disgust, they turned out to be three horsemen riding toward the home ranch, loose and sloppy in the saddle, talking desultorily and laughing. He sat up there above them and watched, vastly disappointed, for they were strangers to him. But it was an indication that the Crownover men drifted homeward in the afternoon. He found a good spot north and west of the big green valley, and waited.

There was no strain in the vigil. Not to a man of Bent Sutton's incredible patience. He didn't smoke or move; just watched, and his reward came when he caught the flash of red sunlight off the cheek pieces of Santa Barbara spade bits heavy with silver inlay. Two riders came slowly, as the others had, but from the west, behind him, following a trail that wouldn't miss his hiding spot a quarter of a mile. He stood up. There was an arroyo they'd have to breach before they could start the incline. He waited until they were lost from sight in it, then stepped aboard the black horse and eased him quickly, at a fast trot, over into the scrub-oak thicket where the trail passed. This time he stood beside the horse with a hand on his nose, ready to stifle any sound. If it wasn't Van Holt it wouldn't make any difference. He would be concealed. If it was — it still wouldn't matter.

But when the riders came up the trail Bent's stare caught and bracketed the distant darkness of the man's lower face, the almost square build of his body in the saddle and the set, harsh expression he was wearing. The other rider was behind Holt. Bent couldn't see him very well and didn't try. He smiled again, but only to himself.

When the horsemen were close enough for him to hear the sound of iron shoes on rock, he looped his horse's reins over a little limb, drew his hand gun and moved up closer.

Holt's eyes had a brooding unpleasantness, and that suited Bent too. The heavily boned face was forceful and dogged-looking, with a hint of cruelty to it. A face, once seen, which was not readily forgotten.

"That's close enough."

Holt's black eyes swivelled without fear and with only a little surprise. He saw the gun first, Bent's face next. He reined up.

Bent heard a quick intake of breath from the other rider. He spoke, looking away. Holt was his shield. "Don't make a move back there." Then he reached up and took Holt's gun, dropped it and held out his left hand. "Give me that lariat."

Holt did. If he surmised — and he must have — what Bent had in mind, he gave no sign of it.

Bent stepped back, still using Holt's horse as a

shield, and nodded his head. "Get down." Afoot, Holt was a good three inches shorter than Bent Sutton, who reached out and pushed him beyond arm's reach. Not until then did he look up and see the other rider. The girl — Antonia Crownover — with eyes as big and as blue as all outdoors, was staring at him in fascinated outrage. He was less astonished than she was, for his surprise was only at seeing her. Hers was over the look in his face and his obvious intent.

"You!" she said.

He nodded before he caught himself, but it made no difference. Mentally he calculated how long it would take her to get to the ranch and raise the alarm. There was plenty of time. He jerked his head sideways. "Ride on."

She lifted the reins instinctively as though accustomed to obedience, then just as quickly dropped her hand again and shook her head. "No. What do you want?"

Bent's glance at Van Holt's back was eloquent enough. He said nothing but looked back at her again. She had lost a lot of color.

"You have no right to be here. This is Crownover range," she said.

He still said nothing, and the words sounded ridiculous in her own ears as well as his. He was wondering whether to let her watch or just to step around and whack her horse. Then she spoke again — to Holt.

"Van? Is he the one you caught last week? You and Dave."

"Yeah." Holt's answer was soft and cold, and he didn't move a muscle.

Antonia Crownover looked over Holt's head at Bent. "That wasn't the first time you'd trespassed — cowboy."

Bent finally spoke. "That's no excuse, lady. Ride that horse on home unless you want to see what happens when the boot's on the other foot."

Her glance grew hot and angry. It locked with the impassive, confident iciness of Bent's look and made no headway. "You'll wish you'd never done this. I'm warning you."

"No," Bent said with no inflection to the words, "not me, lady . . . him. Ride on home. You can fetch him back some goose-grease."

That seemed to her to have some logic. She lifted her reins, and the bafflement and wrath in her glance were knife-sharp and fierce.

When the sound of her going along the far rim of the hillock was dim, Bent gun-walked Holt to the overhang to watch, to be sure she wasn't coming back to use the little Lightning Colt at her hip. He reached out and steered Holt by the scruff of his neck to where the black horse waited.

It wasn't anything he'd ever done before, but he took pains to make it as efficient a gunman's job as Crownover's rider Dave had carried out on him. The black horse probably thought he was dragging a calf to a branding fire — if he thought at all.

Bent finally stopped when the bumping bundle of man back at the end of forty feet of lariat became an inert weight. By then Holt wasn't good to look upon and the black horse was sucking air. Bent got down, trailed his reins, walked back, coiling the rope as he went, and gazed at the unconscious form with rock bruises already beginning to swell and purple. Holt had protected his face in some way. Bent tugged off the lariat and finished coiling it. Laying it very neatly across Holt's chest, he folded his arms over it and went back to horse. He didn't look back until he was a long way off. Then it was a thin-rising cry that split the sparkling late afternoon which caught his attention. He reined up in plain sight on a ridge, twisted in the saddle and looked back. Five riders were pouring around the rim where Antonia had disappeared. They looked like hump-backed ants in single file. The foremost was a much larger bulk of man and horse than the last, which was probably the girl. . . .

And she was probably spitting and clawing mad too. He lingered, thinking of her astonishment at first, then later of her anger, and finally of her warning. That made his features break into the old expression of scorn. A man learned a lot by trying. Ten men after one man wasn't usually the bad odds it seemed. Sometimes — he knew this well — it was the other way around. One man and one good horse could elude a posse because he was prepared; the others were dependent on one another, and one tired man or one lame horse could slow them all.

Bent Sutton had doubled back through some of the best manhunting posses in the West. A bunch of cowboys was never a real threat anyway if a man kept out of rifle range of them. They chased men because it broke the monotony of their daily lives, but let a long ride, a little thirst, some hunger and discomfort and maybe a few long-range carbine shots be hurled at them, and they were glad to go back to their cows.

He sat there until he knew the Crownover men must have seen him if they'd looked at all, then turned disdainfully and rode windingly, carefully, back down across the big plateaus and buttes, the breaks and gullies and great downsloping plains toward Valverde.

Riding, he looked out over the range. Without the infernal wind and dust-laden air, there was a hard paradoxical beauty in the sheer ugliness of the land. More important, it was big. A man could hide out in the Valverde country for a lifetime, and that was more to the point. He tucked that away in a far corner of his mind. There was always such a time for a man who lived by the gun.

He went directly to the livery barn, handed over his horse, left the place and ate at the little café he'd come to patronize, then went back to The Drover's Rest — and felt satisfied with himself.

Jorry Duncan was looking directly at him. It

was dusk and men were in the big room. On instinct he crossed to the narrow little entryway to the card room beyond and stopped in front of Duncan. A quick whiff of breath told him how much liquor Jorry Duncan had drunk that evening. He reeked of the stuff.

"You!" Duncan's voice was thick but his eyes were pretty clear. He licked his lower lip with a quick, snake-darting movement of his tongue. "How long does it *take* you?"

"Not long. I just dragged some sense into his foreman."

Jorry's face paled with an unhealthy rapidity, leaving splotches of liver-color under the sheen of sweat. "You what?"

Bent didn't answer. His disgust became hard and tangible behind the impassive façade of his face.

Jorry jerked around quickly and lunged toward a little door to his office. "In here," he said, and swore a stream of livid words that lingered in the air in his wake. Bent went through the door, closed it and leaned against it. The sounds and vibrations from the barroom came to him through the wood partition. Jorry was sitting crookedly in his captain's chair, hating Bent Sutton for a number of reasons, but mainly because he was acquiring a dread of this killer he had imported and couldn't shake off. He had to look up into the taller man's face again, and that was galling to a short man.

"What did you do? Tell me again."

"Week or so back I was scouting Crownover's range for a chance. His foreman got the drop on me, drug me over the rocks behind his horse. Today I caught him and gave him the same treatment."

Jorry's gasp was a sickly sound. He disliked anything that was openly violent, on general principles. His life — his fortune — had been built upon secretive violence. It was second nature with him.

"They'll come after you." Jorry wasn't concerned over that. He was sick with worry for fear Old Ash or the deadly Van Holt would associate him with Bent Sutton. That would be suicide or worse. He had his own plans. They had once included Bent Sutton. Now they didn't. Sutton appeared as a very dangerous accomplice that must be gotten rid of right away. His very presence, leaning there on the office door with that fixed stare, was anathema.

"Sutton — you've failed. Keep the thousand but ride out of Valverde right away — now. Go get your horse and —"

"Not yet, Duncan. Not quite yet." There was a scornful timbre in Bent's voice.

"But man; they'll come after you!"

"What's that got to do with you?"

Jorry swore at the thought, outraged and more afraid than ever; so afraid he spoke the truth. "Because they might figure you work for me, that's why."

"They won't." His scorn bit deep.

Jorry didn't want to be placated, though. He fought back a desire to walk up and down the room. His color came back, only redder. "Listen, Sutton. Five hundred more if you ride out of Valverde within an hour."

Bent shook his head. "Couldn't now. They'll be coming down this way."

"But they won't know you."

"The girl will. She's seen me twice."

That time Jorry did get up and walk with quick springy steps. "Antonia! Now you've broken everything down."

"What's everything?"

"None of your business. Get out, Sutton. Make a run for it, because they'll hunt you down. I know Ashley Crownover. He never forgets or gives up. He'll hire a gunman to get you." Jorry's voice was rising in a panic of fright that finally left him spent and almost physically ill beside his desk, both hands down, fingers spread and stiff, bracing himself.

"If I was as afraid as you are, Duncan," Bent said, "I'd have left long ago. Why do you want Crownover killed? The ranch? Heck, the girl'll get it."

"She's nothing."

A sudden upsurge of men's voices and the stomping of many spurs out in the barroom made Bent chop off the words. A little spindrift of fear actually did run up his spine, but only because he had a rule that said you should never be caught in a building; always keep a lot of country behind you and a black horse between your legs.

"That's Crownover," Jorry said in a stifled voice.

Bent ignored him, although his glance never left the shorter man's face. He listened to the tumult of many voices and much masculine cursing — with no laughter at all. It would be Crownover's outfit all right, telling of their indignity, with rage on their faces. It didn't mean anything except that he'd have to stay where he was until the small hours. By then the riders would head for home and he could slip out of Valverde with no trouble at all. He nodded his head to Jorry Duncan. Of all the men to be holed up with for five or six hours, Duncan was the last one he would have chosen. Now, though, there was no choice.

"We'll wait them out. Sit down. You're about to fall down."

Jorry didn't obey, but that went unnoticed by the gunman. What stuck in his craw was the fact that now he'd *have* to leave the country before he was able to hit Jorry Duncan where he'd planned to.

"Sit down. We're going to wait them out."

"Are you crazy?" Jorry said. "They'll wonder where I am."

"Let 'em wonder."

Jorry's color heightened. His mock smile was so far lost in fear now that it'd be hours working its way to the surface again. It was all so exasperatingly hopeless where it should have been so simple. A thousand dollars, one shot, and the quick move he'd planned to gain ownership of the Crownover holdings.

Instead he was imprisoned in his own office with a human death certificate in the form of this icy-eyed, motionless, inhumanly blank-faced gunman who'd valued pride above money — and so had made a total mess of Jorry's plans.

He sat finally, and bent his head listening. The tumult had subsided into a steady, harsh drone. Crownover's swaggering riders were staying. That would be because they'd completely lost track of Bent Sutton. He felt a little steadying reassurance. If they couldn't find him, then there was still a bare chance. Better than nothing. If they'd found anything they'd either be out running Sutton down — or beating on his door with their gun butts. Fear tightened his vocal cords until he regained control of himself. He was safe enough for a while, and that recalled the carefully laid plan. The hired killer, the shot from ambush for a thousand dollars, a dead man named Ashley Crownover and the purchase of his holdings from a grief-distraught girl named Antonia. 'Tonia. A fool with a beard wanted her. Well, he could have her. Jorry Duncan wanted the largest, richest, most powerful cow empire in the southwestern uplands — and he would have it.

CHAPTER THREE

Bent stood until his legs were numb; then he went over, got the isolated chair from the corner and carried it back where he could lean upon the wall, watching both Duncan and the locked door. He made a cigarette after a while, when he was sure the bedlam in the barroom wasn't likely to spill over into the office, and smoked it. His eyes were unseeing but his hearing was acute. However, there wasn't anything out of the ordinary to listen to. Just cowboys raising the roof and propping it up with empty bottles. A sound he'd come to know so well it didn't mean anything at all any more.

He stayed like that until Jorry Duncan was a slobber-mouthed, inert little blob of reeking flesh, head down in his arms, asleep and dead to the world. The sounds in the barroom were strained and forced by those loath to leave, now only a very few as the night advanced. But he waited until even those noises died out and the barn of a room was finally in a thralldom peculiar to vacant saloons. He got up, reached down, twisted Jorry's ear cruelly and held on when Duncan's eyes opened in a watery blur of sharp pain.

"Open that safe, Duncan."

Bent left no room for argument. He literally

heaved Duncan out of the chair and to his knees, holding him by the ear. It took Jorry that long to croak out some words.

"What are you doing? There's nothing in there. Let go my ear — get out of here. They'll get you sure if you don't make tracks!"

Bent said nothing but twisted until he could feel the flesh tearing under his fingers and felt Duncan trying hard to turn his head far enough to offset the pain. He turned as far as he could. The muscles of his neck bulged and strained. Bent twisted harder, and Jorry moaned through his teeth.

"All right."

Bent let him go so suddenly Duncan went down on one hand and lifted the other to the side of his head. The sleep was gone out of his face but the puffiness remained. Blinking, with an ache behind his eyeballs, he started to get up. Bent reached out with his boot toe and nudged him — hard. Just that pointed jolt over the kidneys, and Jorry's hands went to work. Bent watched the combination without any interest and stooped only when the little door swung open. Nothing in there?! There were sheaves of green bills tied up with twine. He riffled through them, took four thick bundles and pocketed them, ran two hands over Jorry until he found two hideout guns, both small in size and large in calibre, flung them contemptuously into the safe, shoved the little door closed and twirled the knob. Jorry was staring at the fat-bellied little angel with the green-cloud background; he was rooted, unmoving, burning with helplessness.

"Duncan — one word — *don't!* No matter what you're thinking now — *don't!*"

Bent went out the door, back through the card room into the stygian darkness of a stuffy storeroom. He felt for the rear entrance, found it and let himself out into the lighter, sharper gloom of the hours before dawn. There was a tell-tale chill in the air. Bent moved carefully, watching the litter of refuse that consisted of old discarded wheel spokes, rims, shattered commode pots, bottles of many sizes and shapes, and other unrecognizable and equally useless objects that lay in the way of his route around the buildings, northward.

When he emerged several doors up and across from the livery barn, the town was evidently asleep. Nothing moved as far as he could see. Just the same, he waited a long time before he crossed the road. Then he went into the barn from the rear and used up a lot of time before he reached the stall where his black horse waited with infinite patience.

The man was there, all right, but it was the smell of his cigarette that gave him away, not the movement when he bent his head to douse it; then the deeper blackness of his silhouette, full-bodied, was limned against the lighter darkness. Bent clubbed him down, saddled up and rode out the back way without even rousing the nighthawk. It was still two hours before dawn.

He rode steadily, far east of the main road but paralleling it northward. After sunup he made for the high country where he remembered seeing an ancient trace of another road that had been used for mule trains, more than likely, up out of Mexico. It was the kind of a trail an outlaw never forgot. Never used but usable, all but forgotten and easy on a man's horse — a real back-trail.

He kept on going until he came to the high humped back of the ridge he was circling, and there he stopped, hobbled his horse, squatted in the nooning shade and smoked in lieu of eating. With deliberate slowness he finished the cigarette and, satisfied that no one was coming up the land on his trail, took out the sheaves of money and counted them.

It was a lot of money — more than he'd gotten from most of the hold-ups he had worked at so diligently down along the Border. It made him a rich man. Added to the cache he had — his wilderness bank — it would make him richer than any outlaw he'd ever known. What he liked best about the thought was that the money had come from men who despised him for what he was. Men like Jorry Duncan, and better men. But for Jorry's contribution there was a thin smile of real appreciation. He hadn't gotten it quite as he'd wanted to — he had wanted to do it more subtly — but he'd gotten it, and that would drive Jorry wild. Not because he was outraged at being held up, but because he dared not swear out a warrant. That was the way to hurt a man like Duncan. Hit him in his safe; in his wallet; take his money. Taking his life or pistol-whipping him half to death wouldn't ever make him writhe like taking the only thing he worshiped.

Bent saw slow movement without attaching much importance to it, because it was coming parallel to him, far to the west and from the direction he was riding in. It wasn't pursuit; probably some riders heading for Valverde. He swung his head and watched because he was in no hurry anyway and the two riders were all that moved in the vastness of the rangescape.

The men were riding as though they were on important business, galloping rapidly along the road that led to Valverde. Then they swerved and cut inland. Bent knew the Crownover ranch road lay just over the plateau from them because he'd been over the same ground himself. He was mildly interested. He thought idly it was possible the riders were scouts out looking for his tracks. If so, they were miles wide and going in the wrong direction. He wouldn't be going that way no matter what happened.

Then a small, distant gunshot came whipping into the funnel of distance until it came where he was, so sharp and faint that he stood up, listening for a repetition. None came.

Somebody had been shot down there. Who? Those must have been Crownover riders. Had they mistaken someone else for Bent Sutton? He went over to his horse, tugged up the cincha, toed in and swung up. Whoever it was — it was lucky it wasn't Bent Sutton. He reined back onto the road and started northward. Still wondering ironically if those two Crownover riders had really killed someone thinking it was Bent Sutton, he turned his head and glanced over and down again, as his horse moved on.

The specks were back atop the plateau, only now they were riding as if the devil were behind them. Ahead was a third man, also riding as though his life depended upon it. Bent reined up and watched. The fleeing man was coming straight across the country, a little north but mostly east. He was racing for the safety of the same big hill where Bent was sitting.

There were several other shots, each clearer, more distinct, and closer-sounding than the last. Bent reined around and started the black horse back over his own tracks. He tugged out his carbine and levered it once, riding with the reins loose. He let the hammer down lightly and was careless of the dust banners his horse kicked up until he was plunging, half sliding, half leaping, down a shale incline directly in the front of the fleeing man whose arm was rising and falling as he plied his quirt. There, Bent knelt on the ground, waiting, for he had seen something about one of the two pursuing riders that made him eager to settle a score — a blocky shape with a dark shadow about the lower jaw — a beard. . . .

But it was over before he ever got a chance to

shoot or before the fleeing man even got within range of him. Two fast shots and the man's horse went down in a spray of shallow earth and pebbles. Bent stood up and watched. The rider was catapulted like an old sack, all legs and arms and pinwheeling motion. He didn't even roll when he landed; the fall had been abrupt and crushing.

The thin yell of one of the men made him look up. The rider behind the stocky, massive man was jerking his horse to a sliding, jarring halt. His rifle arm was up and pointing, and Bent could vaguely make out the great O his mouth made. The foremost rider saw him then, too, and reined off so sharply his horse had to lean far over to keep its balance. Bent never got off a shot, didn't even try. The distance was impossible. The men raced away. He watched them until they were small and heading up north again; then he caught his horse, stepped up, eased the carbine back into the boot and rode slowly out to where a dead horse lay in the new sun, being burnished a sweaty copper hue. The figure of a man lay not far to one side of him.

He got down and picked up the man's hand gun. It had silver inlay in the barrel. It also had a firing pin wedged into the firing cap of a cartridge so tightly that nothing short of a rock or a hammer would ever work it loose. He tossed it aside and went over to the still form. The man was big and bearded, with his facial adornment cut off severely, squarely below his chin. His face was square, too, and powerful-looking. There was more than just strength etched in it. There was something perilously like arrogance, or maybe conscious power. Whatever it was, the man didn't look very friendly or pleasant, so Bent didn't waste much time on him. Dead men were no novelty. A broken neck had finished what the two assassins had started, and they wouldn't have had to track him long anyway. He had two frothy marks on his shirt. Two .45 bullets had gone through his lungs. They would have brought down a lesser man long before. This big old devil took a lot of killing, but even a brawny old mountain of a man didn't get up and walk away from a broken neck.

Bent raised his head and looked westward. There was a single rider loping toward him. He gauged the distance, then ignored the horseman long enough to stoop and remove the leather pouch, with its bone buttons, that bulged from the dead man's pants pocket. Inside was money, both paper and silver, and some carefully folded papers. These he opened, shot another look at the approaching horseman, dropped his glance and read. The paper was a signed bill-of-sale for sixteen head of horses, but Bent ignored that. What held his glance was the bold, thick and sprawling signature at the bottom. Ashley Crownover.

Still holding the bill-of-sale, he waited until the rider was close; then his fingers tightened on the paper. That girl again. . . .

She rode up with drawing rein until she saw her father; then she flung herself off her horse and finished the last fifteen feet in a run that left her kneeling beside him. Bent stood like a statue, watching her mouth working. Very gradually, her mumbling dwindled away and she got up and stood facing him.

"Oh, why did you do it?"

Bent was stunned as much by her look as by her words. "*I* didn't do it," he said. Then he froze up inside again.

What she thought was clear on her face. Then she made a primitive noise and flung her hand toward the little gun. But he was quicker. He lunged out, twisted viciously and kicked the gun out across the ground and let her arm go all in one brutally swift movement.

She froze, an ugly look of horror in her wide eyes.

Bent didn't look at the dead man when next he spoke. "Is that your father?"

He got no acknowledgment that she'd heard him; just that same twisted look of soul-deep shock. A movement far behind her caught his glance and he looked, narrowing his eyes against the slanting sun rays. Riders were coming in a pellmell charge. They would be Crownover men, of course. He glanced at 'Tonia again, then over to where her gun lay, before he turned, caught up his reins and swung aboard the black horse. They wouldn't catch him because they'd stop by the dead man. Even if they didn't stop he'd get a good lead. Bent was no novice at eluding people who wanted him. He looked down at the girl again. Misery was in her face. It moved him to speak.

"Lady, I didn't kill him."

One of the men far off let loose with a futile shot. Bent turned and hung in his spurs. He had to keep out of gun range. He rode directly toward the slide he'd come down, picked out a little trail that spiraled upwards and rode up it, feeling the tremendous power under him scrambling and clawing for the top.

When his horse was blowing hard and he was overhead, up where he'd been when he'd first seen the drama of Crownover's murder, he reined up to watch.

The riders were bunched and evidently bewildered. All but two, who were laboriously urging horses already spent on Bent Sutton's trail. He scarcely considered them. He knew which one was the girl by the way she had her back to the men, standing a little apart. He wondered if the shock had passed. His mind slid to something else. Why? There could be only one explanation. Jorry Duncan had sent Holt out to do what Bent Sutton had failed to do.

It would be like Jorry. He was a fox. The more Bent thought about it, the more it looked suspiciously as if Duncan had worked one of his strokes of near-genius.

Crownover's men knew Bent had escaped. They had proof in the departure of his horse and the knocked-out sentinel at the livery barn. They knew, too, that Sutton was against their outfit. Now Ashley Crownover was dead. Bent stiffened in his saddle. It had been terribly close, uncannily close. He had ridden down when he'd seen that one of the pursuers was Van Holt. The girl had seen him and had thought he had killed her father. Damn Jorry Duncan anyway. He had figured ahead as he always did, with that brilliant mind of his. Even riding away, Bent Sutton had nearly been caught — and most certainly had been wonderfully set up for the killing of the wealthiest cowman in the Valverde country.

Bent watched the riders lash the dead man crossways over one of their horses and start back. Two riders rode one horse. They didn't go toward the Crownover ranch, though. They were riding directly toward Valverde; that meant posses. He lifted his reins and plodded onward. The men leading their spent horses after him, toiling up the hot hillside, wouldn't last long. He didn't worry about them. But the law had ways of cutting a man off. Outlaws could thank the telegraph for that.

He rode until the old mule trail petered out on the lowlands. It was dusk. He sought out a place to bed down and made a dry-camp back in the brush and junipers where the sounds of the night would come to him. He smoked and lay back with his head propped upon a rotting stump. A recurrent thought rankled.

Knowing Bent was fleeing, Duncan had gotten

hold of Holt in some way and had sent him to bushwhack Crownover. It was terribly simple, and that was what made it so wonderfully plausible. But where did Holt fit in? There was only one explanation. He and Jorry must be working together toward a common goal — and that worked in nicely too. Holt was Crownover's foreman; he knew better than anyone how much wealth was in the herds, the holdings — maybe even in the banks.

Bent stumped out his cigarette, rolled his head to watch the black horse graze, then looked up at the vault of heaven again. . . .

And the girl thought sure he'd done it. Not that he wouldn't have, two weeks ago. But a slow indignation grew in him now. He hadn't outsmarted Jorry Duncan at all; in fact, it was the other way around. Jorry had set him up beautifully for a crime he hadn't committed. That was what kept Bent Sutton wide awake most of the night: the knowledge that he'd been used and cast aside when he'd thought he'd bested the other man, cut him down to size.

He awakened after a cat-nap, his anger crystallized. He'd go back. He'd try again to outwit old Jorry. The thought brought an uneasy frown to his forehead, because it was contrary to everything he'd taught himself. A gunman never returned. An outlaw kept moving, riding, drifting, so that none could outguess him. But there were things that meant more than safety. Pride was one. He could ride on, but he would never be able to think back without the humiliating memory of Jorry branding him a murderer — outsmarting him when he'd been sure of triumphing over Duncan.

He saddled up the black horse and mounted and sat like a figurine for moments and wrestled with himself. Lifting the reins, he swung down onto the mule trail and rode south, back toward the changeless immensity of the Valverde country.

He rode with bitterness and self-condemnation for companions. He rode also with an automatically functioning instinct of wariness, as a gunman always does — with a wolf instinct. His face was as impassive as ever, but there was a quickening look of shrewdness in his eyes. Bent Sutton, the carefully trained, ever vigilant, coldly unemotional gunman, was a fool; he was going back.

He reined off the trail finally, rode to a little pimple of a hill overlooking the country below, halted, made a cigarette and sat there. Without a plan, except a very vague idea that he would humble Jorry Duncan, he smoked and looked back down the awe-inspiring distances where trouble lay. Riding through the land before, he had missed a lot of its rugged beauty; he noticed that now. Reflective and sanguine, he held the cigarette so that the smoke broke in ripples below his chest. Some of the hardness of the Valverde country came into him; some of the immensity, and the deadliness.

There were no horsemen riding anywhere as far as he could see. No posses. Why?

He spat into his palm and drowned the cigarette's glowing end and dumped it. Why? Well — Jorry Duncan, prime mover and master planner, wasn't interested in whether Bent Sutton was caught or not. All he cared about was his plan. The Crownover riders might hunt for him, but without good leadership that wouldn't amount to much. Sure, there'd be the law from Valverde — but hunting one man in that country was like trying to catch a feather in a windstorm.

The thought came, abruptly, that there was Jorry's blind spot. He thought Bent didn't know he was being used as a murderer's decoy. He had used a man and was forgetting about him. He wasn't interested in what became of Bent Sutton now — only in his own scheme to acquire a huge ranch. Bent carefully dismounted, stood beside his horse and frowned in concentration. What intrigued him was the teasing idea that, somehow, here was his opening. Jorry was no longer interested in Sutton, the gunman. For one thing, that would give Bent access to the Valverde country again. But for what purpose? To block Jorry's plan to get the Crownover place? How? He couldn't buy it, although he had the money. He knew who had killed Crownover, but how could he convince anyone of that?

It made him hot with exasperation. Duncan had tied his hands too well. Better, perhaps, than even Jorry himself knew. And that made Bent's resolve stiffen even more. Guile was one thing he had never tried to learn. He had never before had any reason to. A man with a gun needed no guile. He turned and mounted, rode on slowly with the maddening suspicion that he was outclassed before he even got under way in his fight against Duncan. That added additional incentive to his resolve to fight.

He rode listlessly, but with his inherent caution automatically uppermost. They wouldn't catch the gunman and outlaw, Bent Sutton, by any ordinary means. It would take a Duncan's wiles to do that. Then he thought of the girl — Antonia. There was something there that held his attention. She was between Jorry and the big ranch. He would make her sell. But how did you make a wealthy person sell anything? Holt? Maybe, but Jorry Duncan's way wasn't violence; at least not open violence. Holt was the type to kill, all right — the hard, cruel, dangerously sullen and vicious type. That might be it. Jorry would leave it up to Van Holt to decide what to do with the girl.

Bent had it finally. Jorry had forgotten him; that meant he could move for a while with reasonable safety. Holt would be up to his armpits with the girl and the ranch. Bent Sutton, unexpected, would have a free rein, but he'd have to hit hard and keep Duncan and Holt staggering before they got their feet under them. There was only one way to do that — through the girl.

He dismounted again when he'd reached the

spot where he'd watched the killing the day before, left his horse tied to a juniper tree and went forward to study the trail. Tracks were there; the fact that the two men who had tried to catch him were walking beside their heavy-footed horses told him enough. Afoot, horsemen wouldn't go far. Maybe they'd followed his sign a mile further before they'd given up and gone back. He studied the land again. Far away little banners of dust rose up over by Valverde. The posses wouldn't even get close. He watched them, guessed at their course, swung back up and headed down off the mountain going west, across the path of the oncoming riders but out of sight.

He kept a roving vigil as he was loping across the open flats, heading toward the broken jumble of country far north of the Crownover buildings. There was a lot of sign around. Groups of men had ridden all night, probably, scouring the gullies for him.

He made it safely into the serrated hills and went directly to the highest one on his route. From up there he watched distant specks that were undoubtedly Crownover riders going to and from the grazing ranges. That struck him as odd. How could Holt make things look natural if he didn't send out riders after Crownover's killer? That girl would at least be indignant; at most, she'd fire the coldblooded foreman. Puzzled but not worried, Bent watched all day long. He changed his vantage points often and eventually worked his way within range of the Crownover buildings, and from there he saw the girl waiting while a stiff-acting oldtimer hitched a team to an open buggy.

Springing astride, Bent rode fast in a big half-circle until he was south of the buildings, and the plateau where he'd first seen her was ahead. There, within striking distance of the ranch, he picked his way down into the arroyo and hid his horse by reining him into some clumps of man-high sage and manzanita. With damp clammy hands he sat his saddle, waiting. Now his patience deserted him and with it went a part of his supreme confidence. This was the most insane thing he'd ever done.

The wait was long. Shadows were sneaking out in the arroyo where the ranch road meandered before he heard the buggy coming. He eased forward a little in the saddle, peering through the snarl of spiny limbs, and was poised so that when the vehicle came around the bend, its team going at an easy trot, he was ready. A nudge, and the black left his uncomfortable station and swung in beside the buggy horses. They shied quickly to avoid a collision, and the girl hauled back on the lines to halt them. It happened so swiftly, so unexpectedly, that Bent had jerked the lines out of her hands before she was certain who he was. A stunned look stayed long enough in the blue-green eyes for him to speak into the stillness.

"Wait." He said that because of the Lightning Colt he knew she carried. He didn't especially fear it, but wanted to speak before she tried to draw it. "If you want to go for your gun, all right — but let me talk first. It won't take long."

His words had the effect of jarring her back to normalcy. He could see the way the color ran back under her cheeks.

"Tell me a few things. Why aren't your riders looking for me? Why isn't Holt with a posse? Has Jorry Duncan sent for you?"

She hadn't moved or blinked. He waited until the danger signals in her eyes were flying like battle flags; then he tried again.

"Lady, a man hired me to bushwhack your Dad. That's what I was doing that day you saw me in the windstorm — waiting for him. I never got it done, but that doesn't matter. What matters is that your Dad got bushwhacked, and I'm pretty sure that the same man who hired me is behind this killing."

"You're a liar!" It came with a whiplash expulsion of breath.

He accepted it stoically, never taking his eyes off her face. Before she could shoot he could be on the off-side of his horse. He knew she was close to drawing, too.

"I'm a lot of things," he said, "but not that. All right — you're going to see Jorry Duncan right now, aren't you?"

"No."

That stopped him. "Well, where are you going?"

"To the sheriff's office. He has three posses out. They're after you."

He'd seen two. The fact that a third was around made it all the more urgent that he get out of the canyon and away.

"I won't stop you, but I'll tell you this once more. I didn't shoot your father."

"Then who did?"

He considered the question carefully. There were only four people who knew, and he was one of them. He alone had no reason to keep it a secret. "I can't tell you. You'd tell your sheriff and ruin everything."

"What are you talking about — 'everything'?"

"I want that man too, but for a different reason from yours. I have a stake in this thing you wouldn't understand. That's what I meant."

"More of your lies." There wasn't the same conviction in her voice this time, though.

"No, I'm not lying to you. Why should I?"

"I don't know. That's what I'm waiting for you to tell me." Her glance was sharp but not roiled as before. "You said you were going to kill my father and didn't get the chance. That's enough right there."

Bent had an intuitive flash. Something about the way she used the words made him think of Jorry. "Duncan's already been to see you, hasn't he?"

"He was a friend of the family's."

"When? Last night?"

"Yes."

"Tell me when I'm wrong. He offered to buy the outfit. He said something like — he knew I was out to kill your Paw. That he had men riding the back-country for me. That he'd never give up until I was caught or dead."

"And he won't, either. Neither will I!"

He gazed at her calmly. "I didn't miss much, did I?"

"The only thing you missed was your last chance to get away!"

"I got away, lady, and I came back. Does that mean anything to you?"

"That you're like all killers, that's all." But there was a stirring wonder in the back of her mind. It had been there since he'd first jumped out at her on his black horse. Why? What kept him around? He had a reason, and it had to be strong enough for him to take incalculable risks.

He relaxed a little, watching her face. "If I told you what I saw yesterday you'd call me a liar again. I want you to believe I'm not lying, because I need you, so I'll tell you this. Your riders aren't out after me. I've been watching. They're back on your range. Your foreman may be with a posse — I don't know — but if he told you he sent your riders out, he's a liar."

She didn't answer.

Bent felt hopeless, looking at her. She wasn't going for her gun. She wasn't going to do anything but outwait him, then ride to Valverde and arouse the town. He gathered his reins and held them tightly.

"When you rode over where your father was yesterday — where I was standing — didn't you see two riders riding south like the devil?"

She answered, but it was a long time coming. "I saw two horsemen — yes. Now tell me *they* killed my father."

"No — only one of them did." Listlessness was in his speech and made it slow and low. "Did you see them close enough to notice anything?"

"I didn't look. Didn't pay any attention. I saw you standing there. That was enough."

He would have liked to swear at her because of the solid wall of stubbornness with which she confronted him. He had said all he wanted to say and none of it had amounted to anything.

Then Antonia Crownover spoke voluntarily, and it startled him. "Who were the men? Why would they kill my father? You said you were hired to kill him. What's more damning?"

Anger stirred in his cold blue gaze. "Would I have told you that, if I had killed him? If all I was interested in was killing him — would I still be around?"

"If you couldn't get away."

He snorted in scorn. "Good Lord, lady, you saw me outrun your riders. You know men have been looking for me all night. If I'd just wanted to get away, don't think for a minute I couldn't have."

"All right," she said suddenly, with a quick, short nod of her head. "Why didn't you?"

"I told you. I have a stake in this thing, too."

"What is it?"

"I can't tell you that," he shot back bluntly.

The swift exchange gave him new hope. He leaned forward in the saddle and stared at her. "But if you'll tell me that Jorry Duncan patted your shoulder and said how sorry he was about your Paw — and tried to buy the ranch with the other hand — I'll tell you who killed your Dad."

"He did," she said flatly. "Just about like that, too."

He held her glance and didn't straighten up. When he spoke the words came like gunfire. "Your foreman, Holt. There was another rider with him. I think it was that Dave he rides with — but I won't take an oath about him."

She returned his intent look with one of her own. For a while she didn't speak; then he saw words forming on her lips and waited. They came very slowly, as if she were having trouble forcing them out. "Why did you say it was Van?"

"Because it was." He was puzzled.

"You can't prove it."

"I reckon not," he said dryly, "and he can't prove it wasn't. It's a little late to ask him, too." The last was sarcasm, but she ignored it and shook her head as her eyes finally fell away from his face.

"I don't believe it." There was a pause. "You hate him."

"No," he said, straightening up and casting an instinctive look around at the shadows, "I don't hate him. He isn't worth hating. Maybe you wouldn't believe him if he told you anyway."

She flung her glance back to his face. "Why do you say that?"

"I didn't figure out until now that you might not want to." He lifted a hand to stem the words he saw coming. "Never mind, lady. I want you to promise me something. Or won't you do that either?"

"What is it?"

"That you won't tell a soul — anyone at all — what I just told you about Holt."

She had a troubled expression on her face. Why was this gunman talking like this? Why was he here at all? It didn't make sense. "I suppose," she said in a solemn voice, "that you don't want me to say I've seen you, either."

"I don't care. You can suit yourself there. You have reason to, I reckon — and reason not to."

"What's the reason not to?"

"When you get back home, go ask your riders if they were out counting cattle or hunting for me. You'll have caught Holt in one lie and me in one truth. If he's lied and I've told the truth — then you might want to give me another chance."

She slumped suddenly. Bent saw it, and for the first time he could recall, he felt sorry for a woman. She was confused, bewildered, grieved.

"Ma'am — I haven't lied to you once — not once. If you could believe that, you'd really have a jugful to worry over. If you don't believe me, I want you to give me the chance to prove I'm not lying."

"How could you?"

"Give me your word to say nothing about what I've told you — and give me two days to make good my word to you. Two days isn't much time."

"It's enough to get out of the country," she said tartly.

He ignored it because it hadn't been convincing or showed more than a shadow of her former defiance. "Will you?"

She glanced up from slow contemplation of the hands in her lap. "But you're a killer — a gunman."

"That's Jorry Duncan talking. Whatever I am, I'm not asking you to like me. I don't care about that. I want a chance to wreck the plan of a man who's done me a lot of hurt."

"Jorry Duncan?" Her eyes were wide and liquid and perfectly still on his face.

"Yes."

"You say he was behind my father's death?"

"I didn't say that."

"Yes, you did — practically. That's the thing that's made me listen to you. You were right both times about Jorry, and I don't know what to believe."

"Will you give me the same chance you've given Holt and Duncan?"

"Yes," she said slowly. "I will. I won't tell anyone."

He considered. A battle without communications wasn't worth much. "Then I want you to do one thing more. Remember that spot where I caught you and Holt?"

"Yes; on Juniper Hill behind the valley."

"Day after tomorrow at sunup you be up there." He didn't wait for her answer. He dismounted and handed the team's lines back to her.

He rode the black horse around the team and down over the rock rubble of the gully and up the other side toward the plateau. On the rim he turned in the saddle and looked back, then reined up and watched, doubt growing in him.

Antonia Crownover hadn't turned the buggy and headed back to the ranch as he'd felt sure she would. She was wheeling over the road in the direction she'd been traveling when he'd stopped her — toward Valverde.

CHAPTER FOUR

The secret of longevity to an outlaw is mobility. Hideouts are for novices. Invariably they are caught in them, or killed there. A gunman only uses them when he is injured or in the neighborhood.

Bent had found two such hideouts. One was a lava-blister south of Valverde in a badlands where little grew and less lived. He cached his money there and went to the other place. It was farther south than the lava-blister, and there was a sickly sort of meadow where his horse could feed while he sat on an ancient rocky spire. Squatting up there with the panorama of the country all around him and safe from approach, he could keep his vigil and think. Both were essential.

The day following his talk with Antonia Crownover, he had made a startling discovery in the course of an aimless scouting ride over the tremendously vast Crownover range. The riders he had seen working the Crownover cattle — the men who were supposedly after Old Ash's killer — weren't just riding and tallying. They were gathering, rooting out little bunches of the horned cattle and driving them all to a common bedding ground.

He had watched, wondering, and slowly the

realization came that this was the way Jorry Duncan had planned it. He couldn't buy the girl out; she probably had as much money — maybe even more — than Jorry had. He could break her, though. Especially right now, while she was bewildered and mourning. But Van Holt would have to handle that end of it. Bent watched him all one day at the roundup grounds, making tallies in a little book.

It was so appallingly simple. The cattle would be held in one place; then — some night — they would be rustled. Maybe the Crownover riders themselves would do it. More likely not. But whoever did it wouldn't have much trouble, with the animals all in one place a long distance from the ranch. A ten or twelve-hour start would insure their crossing into Mexico. Lord! It was the simplest, oldest way on earth of breaking big cow outfits.

He had ridden away from the gathering grounds, hunting a place to ponder, and had come up to the lava-blister where the black horse could rest and feed.

He sat cross-legged, smoking and motionless, wondering if the girl had discovered what her foreman was doing. Jorry Duncan wasn't waiting. Bent Sutton was. He stood up and watched the great flaming sun sink away behind the horizon. The night felt warm and there was a good smell of baked earth and running sap in the air. He noticed it as a wild animal would — as a sign that summer wasn't far off. Then he went down to his horse, dragged out the saddle, blanket and bridle and put them on, mounted and rode slowly northeast, up across the badlands toward Valverde — toward Jorry Duncan's town.

The light wasn't strong but it held until he could see the blinking orange of lantern light. He rode toward the village and left his horse with a sinking feeling. A horseman afoot — a wanted man.

There were night strollers that looked like shapes without figures until he was close enough to the far south end of town to make them out. There was a trickle of saddle-back traffic. There were the muted night sounds of Valverde, and there was the sheriff's office below the main section with four horses at the hitchrail. He went as far uptown as that and there he stopped, looking over at the building with its dirty solitary window and its lamp light spilling down the siding, across the plank walk and petering out in the dusty roadway.

A man came striding down from uptown. He had silvery-fine dust on his shoulders, hat, and back. He went into the sheriff's office without knocking and closed the door. Bent had glimpsed a careless looking trio inside, sitting talking. Their attitudes told him a lot. They were bone-weary manhunters, disgusted, dejected and sick of the chase.

He went farther toward the main section and lowered his head languidly when people passed him. Only a handful knew him anyway. Then he saw something that struck a warning note. Jorry Duncan and two travel-stained riders lounged out of the lamp light, talking. Jorry was animated. Bent's glance whipped over him and on to the strangers. He couldn't see their faces but it didn't matter. Their slouched, wide-legged way of standing and the way they both kept a casual vigil over everything around them as they listened to Jorry told Bent they were gunmen.

He turned and went back out of town. What he had in mind hadn't been more than a poor second thought about how to maneuver Jorry out to the Crownover place anyway. Far-fetched, it had seemed better than gnawing inactivity. Now, though, he was inspired. Gunmen meant trouble at Antonia's end of the country and nothing else. Jorry wouldn't hire gunmen to track Bent down. He was done and over with as far as the swift-thinking Duncan was concerned. So there was only one other place for them to go. Crownover's ranch. Bent Sutton wanted to see that the Crownover girl was warned.

He waited on the plateau until they rode by in single file, silent and sinister; then he paralleled them all the way to the ranch yard and swung up to the place she'd called Juniper Hill. There he hunkered, watching the ranch. It revealed nothing.

Jorry was far too wily to be caught at anything, and Bent Sutton was too inexperienced in deceit to catch him. He threw down the cigarette and ground it under his boot heel. He swore in growing restlessness. He stood there for almost half an hour, dreaming up countermeasures and discarding them almost as fast as he thought of them.

He still had his advantage. That alone encouraged him; that and the knowledge that he knew a little — had guessed a little anyway. Having seen Jorry's two newly hired killers, he reckoned that Jorry and Holt were moving, setting up the Crownover ranch for stripping. He swore to himself and spoke aloud.

"All right, what else do I have to know? That's enough."

He spent the rest of the long black hours perfecting his own plan, and by sunup, when he heard a horse coming along the trail below him, he had it shaped to his liking.

It was Antonia on a fat grulla gelding that grunted with every step. He stood up and looked at her. Neither of them said anything for a while, and a sixth sense made him uneasy.

"Bring a posse with you?"

"No."

Her face was as blank as his; watching, waiting, with an awareness that he was there and that was all.

"Did you ask your riders about the posses?"

"Two of them."

"What'd they say?"

"One said, no, he'd been sent back to hunt strays in the breaks west of Slide. That's a part of our range." Her eyes moved a little, probing his face. "The other was Dave Louden."

"Holt's running-mate?"

She nodded. "I really didn't mean to ask him, but it came up when he unharnessed a team for me."

"What'd he say?"

"That's the only reason I came up here this morning. He didn't answer me. Then — last night — he came around to the office and asked for his time."

Bent wanted to swear. "He rode off?"

"Yes."

Well, one of them was gone. Bent walked over closer to her horse and gazed downward. There were men moving sluggishly around the barns and corrals. It didn't matter. Dave wasn't really important. He looked up at her again. She was watching him with that impassivity that didn't seem ever to change.

"Did you order your cattle rounded up?"

"No." A little alarm showed for the first time. Puzzlement was mixed with it. "Why?"

"The way I've felt lately, I put the worst meaning to everything, lady. If you didn't order it, and it's still spring with no reason to bunch and gather and move them to new range — why's it being done?"

She didn't answer him. Instead, she turned her head and looked down into the yard where men were mounting up and where one blocky, massive man stood wide-legged, motioning and speaking. Neither of them could hear his words.

"You don't think I'm telling the truth, do you?"

"Maybe. I don't know." She turned back and looked at him again closely, but with a strained glance. "Jorry Duncan came to see me yesterday forenoon."

"Uh," he grunted. "Why?"

"I'd better tell you something else first. That day when I saw you the first time — in the windstorm — well, I was riding to town for my father to tell Jorry that Dad wouldn't be able to meet him. They were to get together at three in the afternoon."

"I know that. What about it?"

"Well, Jorry knew something Dad had kept from the rest of us. He was losing his sight. He was going blind and I didn't know it. I don't know how Jorry knew."

"He'd find it out," Bent said dryly, but he was startled just the same.

"He — Jorry — knew it. He'd made Dad a proposition to buy the ranch. Dad had thought it over and wasn't going to sell. That day Dad told me all this."

"Wait a minute. Did Jorry know he wasn't going to sell *before* he sent you to town?"

"Yes. Dad had told him so two days before, when Jorry drove out to the ranch. But he'd made the date with Dad anyway. Dad said it was a waste of time to go — especially in that windstorm — and asked me to stop by and tell Jorry he wouldn't be in. I was going for the mail anyway."

Bent nodded. It fitted perfectly. Jorry knew Ashley Crownover wouldn't sell. He had had Bent lay an ambush. It hadn't worked and Jorry, driven by whatever drives such men, had then had Crownover murdered by Holt, and covered it with Bent's flight. He looked up at the girl and smiled. She looked astonished. He told her exactly what he thought, and she didn't lose her surprised look until he'd finished and was wagging his head.

"How the devil do you beat a man that smart?" She said nothing, and he threw up one hand in a hopeless gesture. "The worst of it is that you don't believe me. That's the funny part of it, really, because I'm the only one on your side, and Jorry's got us beat there. With you doubting, my hands are just about tied. He's moving fast, too. Those cattle are part of it. He's hired two more gunmen. I reckon we're hamstrung." He held her glance through a long second of silence; then she broke it with words that had a little fire left in them.

"No, we're not beaten. I told the sheriff last night that I knew you didn't kill my father."

"What?"

"I had to. How else could I draw him off? They'd even sent for a U. S. marshal to help hunt you down. They'd telegraphed to every town north, east, and west of Valverde. I don't care how good you are. Even if you're as good as you think you are — they'd have gotten you. I had to tell him that to make him hold off."

"But why? Why did you do it?"

"Because I don't think you *did* kill my father."

"You've changed a lot, lady," he said dryly.

"All right — then I've changed — but I'm not blind. Twice now Van has told me I have to marry him if I want to hold the ranch together. And Dave quit. He wouldn't say why — just that he wanted his money so that he could ride away that same night. What did that mean except that something was going to happen?"

"Yeah, and soon. He'd know, wouldn't he?" Bent's mind was moving fast. "I'd give a lot to know how many're going to be on that cattle drive."

"Why?"

"How else can we stop them? We have to catch them driving your cattle off with no permission. Lady, that's rustling. That's all we need."

"You want to intercept them?"

"I want to stop them cold. I want to catch Holt a long way out in the country. He'll talk — I'll make him. Remember — *I want Jorry Duncan!*"

"I have five riders."

"Yeah, I know." He looked up at her with a frosty smile puckering the bronzed skin around his eyes. "They'll probably be busy the night the cattle's moved."

She looked genuinely worried for the first time.

"If Duncan got your ranch — would that break you?" he asked.

"No, only in cattle. We aren't poor."

"I reckon not," he said, and then came a thought. He considered it critically, then accepted it wholeheartedly. "I want you to do something for me that I daren't do for myself."

"What?"

"Ride to some other town and send a telegraph to a place called Socorro, New Mexico Territory."

"Not from Valverde?"

He straightened up quickly. "No, not from Valverde. Send it to a man named Amos Fowler, Socorro, New Mexico Territory. Say in it — 'Come to Valverde, Arizona Territory, as fast as you can. Bring friends.' Sign it 'Verde.' "

She was nodding until the last word; then she stopped. He saw her level glance. "The fifth horseman," she said quietly.

His blue glance was questioning. "The what?"

"You're the Verde River Kid." It wasn't a question.

"I am."

"My father used to say you were the fifth horseman."

"That doesn't make sense."

"Doesn't it? Did you ever hear of the Four Horsemen of the Apocalypse?"

"No. What about them?"

"They were — well, it doesn't matter."

He waited for her to go on, but she didn't. He had no idea what she meant and that irked him a little, but he didn't show it. She straightened up in the saddle suddenly and looked away from him to where the early sun was bringing new light and life to the country. "I could ride over where they've gathered the cattle and make Van tell me — couldn't I?"

"I doubt it," he said. "You could ride over and find them all right. That wouldn't be hard. But you'd have a devil of a time making him tell you anything, and you might ride into something you weren't looking for."

"What?"

"I don't know. Anyway, you're talking like a fool. If he's let you have the run of the place so far, don't push him. You're lucky. Let it ride like that."

"I'll go to Centerville and send your telegraph. When do you think they'll move the cattle? I mean, will your friend be able to get here in time to help?"

"I don't know. I can delay the cattle drive a couple of days, I think."

She looked down at him with a frank gaze that had none of the old antagonism in it. "Will you tell me something?"

He knew what was coming and shook his head. "No. Not now or ever. Why I want Duncan is my business. Let's leave it like that."

"All right." She looked away again. "My father's funeral is tomorrow."

"Will your cowhands go to the funeral?"

"Yes, the town is making a fiesta of it. Everyone's going. Why?"

"Nothing. Just wondered. All right." He turned away abruptly, went back and got his horse, swung up and turned with a quick chop of his head that was the closest he'd ever come to telling her good-bye, and rode away. He was too far lost in thought to make another meeting date with her.

He rode steadily until he was far around Valverde back by the lava-blister. He stayed there only long enough to make sure no one had tracked him, found his cache, then went still farther south to the little valley where he unsaddled, hobbled his horse and crawled back up to his old vantage point. There he smoked, digesting a lot of things, and waited for the day to die.

He ate some venison he'd shot two days before in the little meadow, rolled up in his poncho and slept atop the stony upthrust until just before dawn. Then he saddled up once more and cut around through the low places until he was west of Valverde and close to a juniper-studded knoll. From up there he watched riders trooping into town from the outlying ranches. He waited until a few grew into a stream of riders and buggies; then he slouched and kept his vigil until the stream died down to a trickle of latecomers. Then he rode due north, right up through the Crownover range, west of the buildings and the big green meadow, north over the increasingly rugged country.

He rode past the place he surmised was known

locally as Slide. There, a huge granite hill had been eroded through the centuries until one half of it had sheered off and gone down into the canyon with a roar that must have carried over miles of prehistoric countryside. He watched for riders all the way and saw none. But when he was close to the bedding ground, he used his natural caution. The noise of a big herd off to his right came faintly at first, then louder. When he caught the smell he knew he was close.

Winding his way downward to a fringe of trees near the valley floor where the animals grazed, he sat motionless, watching. It was possible there was a guard. One man couldn't have held that herd, but he could and would be handy, should anything arise that the intelligence of a man might avert — a stampede, for instance.

The sun wasn't down in the valley yet except along a far western slope where a few critters poked among the rocks. He waited a long time. Wherever the rider was — if there was one — was out of sight. Bent squirmed a little and cast a long last look over the countryside. Nothing showed but cattle. He shrugged his shoulders. He rode far up around the west side of the cattle and kept right on going until he'd made a complete circle. There was a lot of horse sign, but he didn't see a man anywhere, nor was he hailed, in spite of the fact that he'd deliberately ridden in plain sight most of the way.

Below the herd, eastward, he turned and watched the farthest cattle graze. The ones he'd passed had trotted down into the meadow and were standing like deer, wicked horns held high, watching him. Slowly he rode toward them without a sound. They kept their heads toward him, and others caught his scent. Their uneasiness was spreading. He had his hand gun in his lap, riding so that the animals trotted a little way ahead of him.

As the cattle drifted westward away from him toward the hills beyond the valley, Bent eased forward. The black horse took his cue and went into a quick lope. Bent went straight at the closest bunch of reddish bodies, flung his hand gun high and snapped off a shot. As though awaiting some such signal, the cattle broke. Panic spread. They ran, some bellowing for calves that could outrun a fast horse. Others threw themselves at the hillside. Bent reined up. It didn't take more than that to stampede longhorns; that was why they had to be handled with such care and caution.

He sat and watched. The writhing sea of hides toiled up the hills and out of sight. Some broke off from the main herd and went instinctively toward the places where they had grazed and bedded down over the years. Bent turned and rode northwest so he'd be able to overlook their flight. The black horse wound around the hills until he was atop a knoll churned dusty and rancid by the hooves of wild cattle. Bent reined him up and smiled. The cattle were specks of moving color against the pristine brightness of the land. They were distant and small. He nodded to himself and rode away, heading south again. Fortunately he was high up when he saw the two hard-riding men spurring from the general direction of the ranch.

He reined up and watched them. Evidently they had heard or seen some cattle. Maybe some homing bunch had fled toward the ranch. The riders would know the entire herd had gotten away — been spooked — if they saw part of them running, red-eyed and with lolling tongues. The two riders were the two men Jorry had been talking to the night before.

They were using a well-worn trail. He swung around and hooked the black horse. There was no great need for hurry, but he hurried anyway. He unshipped his carbine and held it loosely in his right fist as he rode. He hadn't wanted Jorry to know he was back in the battle up to his shoulders — but now he did. There was something unappealing about the way he'd worked up to now. He preferred to fling his challenge down before Duncan in plain sight. The trail went along a side-hill and angled down to a little arroyo, then worked its way around a large, outthrust boulder higher than a man on a horse and half buried in the earth around it. Bent knew a strategic spot when he saw one. He made for the place and slid the horse, dismounting on the fly. He was set and ready when he heard the running hooves of the oncoming riders slacken to a trot, as they slowed to go around the big boulder.

Then he stepped out with the carbine cocked and as steady as his eyes were.

"Haul up, fellers."

The first man's astonishment was so great he jerked too hard and his horse stumbled, recovered himself and bunched under the saddle, aquiver. The second man's hand was going down when Bent hollered:

"Don't!"

It worked; the man froze. There was something familiar about him, but Bent couldn't place it and didn't try very hard right then. With the same speed that had given him the upper hand, he bobbed the carbine's snout curtly.

"Dump the guns, boys."

They did, but by then their amazement was wearing off. Bent studied them closer. "You Crownover riders?"

"Yeah," the foremost rider said. "Who're you?"

"I'm not a liar like you are, pardner. You're no more Crownover riders than I am. Jorry Duncan pay you yet?"

"What are you talking about?" the second rider said, his eyes holding an intent sharpness. Bent had the feeling that the man recognized him and was trying to give him a name. "Did Jorry Duncan — the saloonman in Valverde — pay you yet?"

"What'd he pay us for?"

"For heading some stampeding Longhorns toward Mexico," Bent said with an edge in his voice. "Don't balk on me, boys — I'll shoot you off those horses quicker'n a flash. Answer up."

The foremost rider nodded his head. "All right, cowboy; Duncan paid us. You satisfied?"

"Sure, I am if you are. How much apiece?"

"Six hundred — and we ain't got it with us."

"Course not," Bent said. "Now — how would you like to make twelve hundred apiece for *not* running the Crownover critters?"

The second rider's face gradually creased into a wry, unpleasant smile. He gave a little dry chuckle. "Huh! I know you now. You're the Verde River Kid. Seen you in Socorro."

Bent eyed the man distastefully. He knew the breed inside and out; treacherous, totally undependable and unpredictable. Not real gunmen, actually; just killers. Whiskey killers at that — hard drinkers.

"Yeah," he said. "Now — you want that twelve hundred or not?"

The second man's smile broadened. He answered as Bent had known he would. They all figured the same way. "Twelve hundred added to six hundred. That's eighteen hundred, Marty. We're gettin' paid by both sides. I like that. All right, Kid — you're the boss. Where's the money?"

Bent had it. He counted it out and handed it to the first rider. It didn't leave him much, but he had the cache to fall back on, and money wasn't any good to him in the Valverde country anyway. The second horseman leaned far forward along his horse's neck with his hand outstretched. The first rider laboriously counted out half the money and passed it back; then he faced forward and crammed the bills into a pocket with a lopsided smile at Bent.

"No sense in us stayin' around now, is there, Kid?"

Bent had been thinking. "No — not unless you want to earn another thousand."

The men both grinned wolfishly at the same time. The second one, with a sudden camaraderie born of respect for the man on the ground and greed — laughed and swore some sizzling oaths.

"You want Duncan kilt?"

"No," Bent said. "When were you supposed to take the cattle south?"

"Couple days. Holt said he'd let us know. This Duncan sent us out t' the ranch t'other night. Holt was cussin'. He ain't got his line-up b'low the border all set up yet. We was waitin' f' that. Ought t' have word today, maybe t'morrow."

Bent nodded. "Well — I just stampeded them. You'll be rounding them up again for another couple of days. For a thousand dollars more you boys stall him for as long as you can. Make hard work of gathering 'em. You know — drive 'em farther back so's the Crownover riders will have a time finding them."

"Sure. Slow 'em down for three, four days. That's easy." The gunman's long, perpetually squinted eyes were full on Bent. "Mind us askin' what's your end of this business?"

Bent gave the man a cool stare. "A thousand dollars ought to keep you from worrying about me too much," he said.

The other outlaw laughed, but the speaker didn't look abashed. He nodded his head and shrugged. "You're the boss, Kid," he said. "When'll we pick up the other thousand?"

"I'll bring it to you at the ranch."

"At the ranch?"

"Yeah. About three days from now."

The riders were studying him closely. The one who had recognized him inhaled a big breath and let it come out noisily.

"Don't worry, boys. When I come I'll have your money and no one'll stop me — not Holt or his Crownover bunch."

"Oh. Well, say — you ain't comin' with the law, are you?"

Bent grinned for the first time. He didn't answer the question. The grin and wag of his head was assurance enough for both the nightriders.

"All right, Kid. We just stall 'em for three, four days — until you show up. Nothin' else? We could fetch you this Duncan if you wanted — or this feller thinks he's so tough — this Van Holt with the chin whiskers."

"No — just do like I say and keep your mouths shut. Keep an eye on Holt. If he looks like he's getting ready to ride — just sort of keep him around. I don't think he will, but you can't ever tell. I don't want him around the Crownover girl, either."

That was something they understood, but only their eyes showed it. "Sure, Kid. The cattle an' the girl an' Holt. We'll do it. You goin' to take care o' this Duncan shrimp yourself?"

"Yeah, and I'll give you another five hundred if Holt makes it hard for the girl before I get back and you boys yank the slack out of him."

The second gunman's eyes widened and he smiled at the same time. "Marty, a man could get rich around these parts."

Before the man called Marty could answer, Bent said, "Or dead, depending on how he handles himself."

"Kid — for that kind of money you got real friends."

Bent nodded. "I hope so, boys. I'll have lots of tracking-down time when we're through here. All right; go on. You'll find the cattle scattered to hell an' breakfast. Holt'll be fit to be tied. He go to the funeral?"

"Yeah. Everyone went but us. We're new hands so we didn't have to. Holt didn't like the idee but he had to. Seems the girl's actin' a leetle bronko, and he wanted t' sort o' settle her down again."

Bent stooped and handed them both their hand guns, watched them from a leaning position over the carbine as they holstered them and looked up, waiting. He had nothing more to say, so nodded his head and stepped back off the trail. They each dropped him a nod, a grin, and walked their horses on by.

He got back into the saddle and shoved the carbine into the boot. Whatever else he did, now he'd have to go back to the cache and count out three thousand dollars more. The thought of spending the money made him smile. The money he had given the gunmen, as well as the other three thousand, was Duncan's money. So Duncan's money was being used to pay the gunmen he had hired to rustle the cattle, and his hirelings were going to double-cross him.

That paid Jorry back for using Bent Sutton as he had.

Bent rode southwest, far enough to avoid meeting any returning riders, and his smile lingered.

CHAPTER FIVE

Bent killed one entire day just watching the Crownover riders scouring their huge range and driving cattle back to the holding ground. There was something about the way they did it, alone, in pairs and in groups, that made Bent want to chuckle. They were angry. They were doing a job over again, and that was something no man enjoyed.

He watched Van Holt make his tally again, the reins hanging loose, his horse hip-shot and drowsing as the man on its back toted up columns of figures in the little tally book.

Bent knew Crownover range well enough now so he could avoid being seen closely enough for the riders to identify him. He watched the two gun men ride together. They went farther than the others, and usually one would stay upon the ridge while the other one would spook little bunches of cattle farther back into the breaks and badlands of the range.

He felt a lightness of heart such as he'd never felt before. This was a new kind of game to him. It wasn't like stopping a stage or robbing travelers or running off bands of prized horses in the night. This was using wiles against a man whom Bent Sutton had known as one of the wiliest men in the far reaches of the frontier. It gave him a sense of exhilaration nothing else ever had.

He rode leisurely back southward and caught the distant outline of a motionless rider over on Juniper Hill where he'd met the girl.

He rode slowly, his eyes a little above the figure of rider and horse, getting a better perspective. What made him certain was the blue bandana under the up-curving hat. It was the girl all right. He waved his arm at her in an overhead motion. She didn't wave back, just moved out on her horse and followed the trail she was on. He didn't want to be that close to the ranch right then.

Riding so as to converge with her trail, he waited a mile farther south. When she came up it was astride the same fat grulla horse. He could hear the animal's breathing before she ascended the last hill and stopped close to him, very sober-faced and big-eyed.

"Did you stampede the cattle?"

"Yes'm. Did Holt tell you they were gathered?"

She nodded. "Yes, he told me, but he said it was because we needed an accurate tally."

Bent grinned. "Sure; you can't sell a big herd unless you know how many you're selling."

She made a little motion with one hand. "That doesn't matter."

"The cattle?" he said, surprised. "Well, they represent a heap of money."

"Yes," she said. "Money," as though it were an abstraction. "I sent your telegraph."

"Thanks. Did you know you have two new riders?"

"No."

He looked steadily at her and gradually understood something. Jorry wasn't far wrong at that. This girl couldn't run a ranch as huge as the Crownover outfit. "Does Holt do all your hiring and firing and so forth; handling the cattle and all?"

"Of course. He's the foreman. Those're his jobs."

"Oh." He felt as if he'd stumbled into an ambush. It was a little embarrassing not to know the rudiments of the only industry in the land.

"Didn't you ever work on a ranch?"

"No'm. Never had to."

"I suppose not," she said, and immediately regretted saying it. She blushed a little and groped for a quick way out. "Jorry drove back with me from Dad's funeral."

"That so?"

Her glance was perfectly solemn, almost lugubrious. "Yes. He told me you'd been caught and hanged at Fallen Leaf, over in New Mexico Territory."

Bent was startled. He didn't speak, so she went on again.

"That's why I was up on Juniper Hill today. I was there last night, too."

"Waiting for me?"

"Yes."

It was too ridiculous. "First off, lady, Fallen

Leaf's a long way from here. I couldn't have ridden that far since I saw you last if my horse had wings. Second place . . ." Then something struck him. She had actually thought he had fled. Not being trusted wasn't anything new, but this time it made him feel decidedly indignant, for some reason. His face took on a cold, flinty look. "You believed him, I reckon?"

"I don't know what to believe any more."

The quiet, calm way she said it made him pull back his head just a little to get a better look at her. "Why?" he said, without knowing why he said it.

She let her glance shift just enough so that she was looking over his shoulder. Instantly he swung his head around. There was nothing back there but Valverde country, always the same. A little irate, he swung forward again when she started to speak.

"Why does Jorry want the ranch so badly? Do you know?" she asked.

"Jorry couldn't answer that himself. It's something inside him."

"He does, you know. He wants it very badly. You were right. Not in what you said, but in what I figured out from what you didn't say." Her eyes went back to his and stayed there. "He and Van are very close."

"So?"

"So Jorry must know that Van's told me I have to marry him if I don't want to lose the ranch."

"You didn't tell Jorry that, did you?"

"No, of course not."

"Just asking," he said defensively.

But she didn't pay any attention to what he said. "Why does Jorry want the ranch? Why does Van want to marry me?" Her glance lost some of its perplexity. "Why are you after Jorry Duncan?"

He grunted under his breath. "I can't answer the first one any better'n I already have, but I'll add this much: Jorry Duncan's been like that all his life. Whatever he's had — he's wanted more. It's made him rich — sure — but it's going to kill him, too."

"You'll do that, won't you?"

He ignored the remark. "It's something that lives inside a man — like pride, I reckon. I don't know exactly, but I know most men have it."

"Does that apply to Van, too?"

He considered, then nodded. "I reckon. Maybe with him, it's wanting to own something he'd never get any other way — a wife that's rich and a ranch that's the biggest. He's hard to figure out in some ways."

"All men are," she said.

"No, not all of them, lady."

"You aren't?"

His guard went up instinctively. "I'm not in it like they are."

"Yes, you are. More so, even. If you hadn't come along — it'd all be over and done by now."

"Not yet," he said, "but they'd have gotten away with a lot, maybe. You can't tell."

"You still won't tell me why you're in it, though, will you?"

He thought he'd steered the conversation around this but she hadn't been fooled. He shook his head. "I told you before I'd never talk to you about that."

"I know." Her voice was small, defeated. She was silent for a moment, and he took advantage of it to change the subject.

"Those two new men you don't know about — Jorry hired 'em and sent 'em to Holt. He put 'em on as riders. They were supposed to do the actual running of your Crownover critters to Mexico."

That brought her glance up again with a glint of sharpness in it. "How do you know?"

"I talked to them."

"You knew them?"

It irritated him. "No — I didn't know them. One of them knew me, though. Anyway, they aren't going to rustle your stuff. They're working for me — for you and me — now. And another thing — as long as they're around, you don't have to worry about Holt."

"No?"

The quizzical way she regarded him when she said it made him balk from saying the rest of it. "No," he said, and that was all.

She didn't push it. "Now what?"

"Wait a couple more days. I've got some plans that'll pretty well cinch things — I hope, anyway."

"Those men from Socorro?"

"Yeah."

Then she staggered him so that his impassivity almost fled. "Kid, you don't believe in anything, do you? You don't believe in decent people or things like love and respect, do you?"

He was too surprised to answer.

"My father knew men like you. He told me he knew a lot of them when he was younger."

Bent thought back to that dead, harsh face, and believed it fully. He also recalled the little fragment of information Mort Emmons had told him over a sour-mash drink one time, about Ashley Crownover coming into the Valverde country in a hurry, thirty years before.

"He told me gunmen are two kinds of men. Maybe I should say two kinds of men make gunmen. No — that isn't right. Well, anyway, he knew about you. Everyone does, I reckon. You've made your name well known. He said you were either a born outlaw or a made one. He said a man could tell which if he ever got to talk to you. Made outlaws are vicious; they drink and run wild because they can't conform — won't conform — to the way the rest of us live. The other kind — the born outlaws — never have a chance to be anything else. Dad said they're the worst kind because they kill and rob the way a wolf does — to go on living. He said they weren't easy to kill unless they rode with others. If they're lone wolves, then they usually couldn't be killed. He knew, too. He knew a lot about badmen."

"I reckon he did," Bent said suddenly; then he bit back the rest of it. No point in saying it. The old devil was dead, and she was hurt enough by that. But he wished he'd met him alive for a few minutes — first.

"You're a lone wolf, Kid. You don't believe in anything. You're a born outlaw. You've never worked on a ranch — you told me that. You've always been an outlaw." Her eyes were very steady on his. "Why? Tell me; I want to know."

"You want to know too much," he said bluntly. "Figure it out from what your Dad told you." He let the words blast into the short distance between them, then jerked his horse around and rode off.

She watched his back for a second. "Kid?"

He didn't turn or speak or even slacken his horse's stride.

She turned her horse finally and went back along the little ledge of a trail that wound down through the gullies and across the knobs of hills until it fetched up in the Crownover ranch yard. Maybe she'd never fully understand men such as her father had been and the Verde River Kid was, but they were exactly like the Valverde country, and she loved that, too. . . . There was a challenge in it.

Bent rode southward until he was on a lip of land that overlooked the quick-dropping swale that separated the grazing country from the vastness of the broken, flinty lava beds that lay across the way, bleak and inhospitable to every man who rode by them — except outlaws — men like himself.

Horsemen were riding lazily — three of them. He reined up and watched. He couldn't cross the swale until they were past. They were small and riding from the direction of Valverde. He waited for them to pass by, and he thought of the things Antonia had said, and the reflective way she had said them. She'd been thinking — that was the trouble with women. Her own affairs were in jeopardy, and she'd been wondering about him.

One of the horsemen rode off a little, apart from the others. Bent watched him with a curious stare. The man kicked his horse into a lope and held his reins hard to the right, snugged back above the rider's belt buckle so that his horse, its neck arched and head held in, loped in a tight little circle. Bent's anger was washed away by surprise. "I'll be darned," he said aloud. The black horse flickered his ears before he responded to the spurs and went down the sidehill in a sliding, trotting rush.

"Amos — you old devil — haven't been so glad to see your scrawny face in years."

The wispy, deeply tanned man shook with pleasurable laughter and looked around at the two younger men, who were grinning. "Lord a'mighty, Kid — we been ridin' this country like Injuns all day, makin' signals. Where'n tarnation you been hidin', anyway — and what fer?"

Bent leaned forward and shook hands. "Soapy, you look as good as ever. A. J., I'm sure glad to see you boys. Your old man never wasted any time, did he?"

Amos Junior (A. J.) had a long, fierce-looking knife slash across his left cheek. Unsmiling, he was a dangerous-looking man. Smiling, he was a boy grown tall. Soapy was pig-eyed, like his father, and there was a laziness about him a man felt rather than saw. Old Amos Fowler, though, was easily identified for what he was. The country had lots of them. Old Confederate soldiers in whose hearts the fire had never been quenched. The devil Quantrill and the hero Moseby had taught them a trade of plundering Yankees they couldn't relinquish.

Amos' eyes were shrewd and steady; level eyes that asked nothing and offered no excuses. "What'd you fall into, Kid?"

"Trouble. Come on — I've got a cache over here in the lava beds. I'll tell you."

He did, both while they rode and later, while they sat and smoked and let their horses graze boldly in plain sight of anyone who happened along southwest from Valverde.

Amos handed around some jerky from a burlap pouch that left brownish grey fibres indented in the meat. They all ate it. Amos cleared his throat twice and spat, then twisted out his cigarette. "All right, that'll be easy, Kid. But it'd be a whale of a lot simpler just to drag so-called Jorry Duncan out here and talk to him for a spell, then hunt up a lynch limb and leave him danglin'." Amos shifted gingerly on the hard rock and made a wry face. "What a country! Well — all right, son — we'll do it your way. You got the stake in it anyway. When you want to ride?"

Bent chewed thoughtfully. "When did you boys get here?"

" 'Bout foah this mo'nin', I'd say," Soapy answered.

Bent shrugged. "No great hurry. Let's ride over to a little meadow I know about and get some rest. Tomorrow's plenty soon — tomorrow just before sunup."

They went to the little meadow and turned their horses out. They talked until early twilight, then rolled over and over in their folded saddle blankets and went to sleep.

Bent awoke long before dawn. His mind was functioning almost before his eyes were open. The situation was changed now. He wasn't a desperate lone man against a country and its people. At their worst, the Fowlers were worth ten like the two gunmen he'd bribed away from Jorry. They were shrewd, hard, relentless men, formed, forged and sustained by their environment — the kind of friends a man sought and very rarely ever found.

So he had the Fowlers and the two hirelings he didn't need, but who had served their purpose anyway. The thought made him smile. He was getting to think like Jorry Duncan. The smile died swiftly. Maybe it wasn't a coincidence. That brought him up out of his bedroll, and he looked into the shallow, pale gloom of pre-dawn.

The situation had changed. The cattle wouldn't be rounded up and bunched for at least another day. Jorry still didn't know who — if anyone — he was fighting, except 'Tonia Crownover. Holt, whether he had any suspicions or not, wouldn't know what was going to come rolling into the Crownover ranch yard within a few hours. Everything pointed to one thing — the finale.

He stopped, felt around for his boots and pulled them on. The spur music he made brought three heads up at once. "Dawn a'ready?" someone asked in genial complaint.

"No, not yet," Bent said. "I'm going down to drive the horses in a little closer. There's a creek yonder when you want it."

He walked out across the ankle-high feed and felt the dewy-dampness seep through the pores of his boots and chill his feet. It made him conscious of the feed in the country, the immensity of it, the monotonous sameness and agelessness. He stopped when he saw the silhouettes of horses ahead of him, and looked up and around, over the lava beds to the south and the good feed country to the north and west and east.

"Funny how a country can make a man aware of it," he said aloud, after the fashion of men much alone. "Funny how a world of rock and hills and prairies can seep into a man's guts like the dew seeps through his boots." Then he thought of something else.

"You don't believe in anything...." He let his mask settle. "The devil I don't. Every man does. I believe in this — and in me. That's all. The country and me. What else is there?" He looked over at the horses. "A big country like this, that black horse — and this gun. What else should I believe in? Your God and your respect and your love?" He was going to say something harsh, and didn't because a quick tightening in his throat stifled the words. For a moment he stood without moving; then he started toward the horses in a flat-heeled walk, setting each foot down hard and solidly so that the animals heard him and looked up and waited.

He led them back to camp and smelled the fire. Old Amos was cooking something. Bent smiled a little; not a wholehearted smile but an understanding one. Old Amos was always hungry. The skinny old devil was all rawhide and recollections from The War. Amos had taught Bent a lot, during those long days at his stump-ranch hideout over in the mountains behind Socorro. There was a lot he hadn't ever taught him, too, because Amos — ever smiling — didn't believe in a lot of things, and what he did believe in he didn't believe should be laid out like a book for other back-trail riders to stare at and turn away from.

"Ever stew up jerky with mustard greens, Kid?" The little faded eyes were always the same — frank and interested.

"Never did, Amos." Bent looked over at A. J.

and Soapy and grinned. "Did you?"

"Oh, heck, yes. Lots o' times, boy. You'd be s'prised what a man'll eat sometimes. When you think back on it later, it's enough t'make you want to heave it up."

"Well," A. J. said in his drawling way, "why'nt y'give us a taste? The smell's awful — th' taste couldn't be any worse."

Soapy got up from his hunkering position and went toward the horses. "Kid, y'know this country pretty well?"

Bent nodded. "Yeah. I've ridden it from hell to heaven and back."

"Good; soon's Paw's filled up with that bait he's a-makin', you lead us, huh?"

And that was the way they rode out, with Bent in the lead and Amos bringing up the rear, making soft, comfortable belching sounds that bubbled in his throat, the two boys laughing at him as though danger didn't exist for any of them.

Bent led them due north; then he edged east a little and kept going at a shuffle-footed walk until they were high above the Crownover ranch — up on the trail he'd dragged Holt over. Bent paused a moment before he swung over onto the downward trail and eased forward with the reins. Soapy, behind him, made a whistling sound.

"Who'd ever a-thought they was such a place? Paw, look at that meadow."

Amos mumbled something and fell back into silence. There was something about naked country that made him uneasy. A man didn't ride over it without knowing a bullet from a hidden gun could kill him before he ever heard the noise or saw the flash. His country was brushy, with deer trails and lots of prickly growth, and a man never worried much about being exposed when he rode it.

Bent was watching the buildings as he rode. A little weak light filtered from the bunkhouse, but aside from that the place was dark. When he came off the trail into the hard-packed yard, he reined up a second, then went forward again.

He rode across the yard, listening to the sounds of their horses. The others came up beside him in silence, like dark avengers on horseback, unsmiling, wolf-wary and erect in their saddles. He watched the bunkhouse light as he rode toward it. Van Holt was going to be surprised.

They tied up and left their horses. There were little spur sounds in the stillness. Four tall men moved toward a weathered door. One of them lifted the bar and shoved inward with his scuffed boot toe. The light spilled out into the raw darkness before dawn, glanced off four hard faces covered with beard stubble and down over bodies whipcord lean and fit.

Bent stepped through the opening so the Fowlers could edge in. Nine heads with stunned faces turned and stared, frozen by astonishment. Some were stepping into pants, and others sitting tugging on boots. One blocky, black-eyed man was fully clothed, and his van dyke beard was combed out neatly below an ugly mouth.

"Just stay that way, boys, just like you are." Bent made no motion toward his gun and neither did the Fowlers. The odds were against them.

Bent's glance moved toward Van Holt. "It isn't going to work, Holt. I reckon your friend Dave knew it when he rode off."

Holt swore a clipped word of defiance. "You got a lot of guts coming around here after killin' Old Ash."

Bent answered as smoothly as before. If there was anger or resentment inside him it didn't show in his face. "You trying to convince yourself, Holt, or your riders? You know who killed Crownover, and you know it wasn't me."

Soapy and A. J. moved around Bent and never once crossed in front of him. Their father was leaning a little to one side of Bent, his face unsmiling but pleasant-looking, his little eyes like chips of agate.

"What you doing here, Sutton?"

"Came for a talk. Why didn't you tell Jorry I'd dragged you?"

"I didn't have to!"

Old Amos gave a brittle chuckle and wagged his head. "Tell me somethin', mister. Where do all you boys with beards get the idee you're so tough?"

Holt's black glance flickered to the older man but he didn't answer him. Soapy and A. J. had the guns piled on an empty upper bunk. They were standing back against the rear wall, watching and listening. Soapy's lazy look had disappeared. In its place was alert interest.

"All right, Holt. When are you going to move the Crownover cattle?"

Holt's face tightened. "You got a lot of savvy, Sutton. Answer that yourself."

"Sure," Bent said. "Today or tomorrow. No later'n day after tomorrow." He shot a sidelong glance at the two traitorous gunmen who were standing motionless among the others, wondering what their part in this was to be.

The foreman reddened. "You got a long nose, Sutton."

"Long enough," Bent said. "Well, you aren't going to move the critters at all."

Holt's flush deepened. He was perilously close to the drawing point. He would fight, Bent knew that, but not against four-to-one odds.

Holt relaxed a little. "Sutton, you're smart, real smart. The biggest mistake you made was when you hung around this country after you killed Ol' Ash. If that's the way you wanted it — all right. Now let me tell you something." He stopped, and the dark shadows in his eyes deepened.

"You think Jorry don't know you're around. He does, mister. What do you think of that?"

Bent was surprised but not worried. Not until he'd turned it over in his mind a little; then he saw cause for uneasiness. Jorry Duncan was smarter than any man he'd ever run across. He leaned back against the wall and waited.

"Y'want to know how he knows? I'll tell you. Because 'Tonia went to the law in Valverde the day after her old man got it, and said you didn't kill him. That mean anything to you?"

"Not a thing," Bent said brittly.

"It did to Jorry. He figured if she was protectin' you that you'd talked to her, an' if you'd talked to her — you was still around."

"What made him think that? She could've been guessing."

"Yeah," Holt said tartly, "she could've been — only she wasn't. You saw Ash killed. Others saw you standing over him, remember?"

Bent knew Holt was telling the truth, because he knew Jorry that well. "All right, what's the rest of it, Holt?"

"There isn't any — blast you. You dealt yourself in — now see if you can drop out."

"You think I'll run? Do I look that scairt of Jorry Duncan — as you call him?"

"You can't run, Sutton. No place left to go. While you've been doggin' the Crownover outfit, he's had trackers on your trail. The country's plumb closed off, Sutton — so try to run if you want to."

Jorry, knowing, had planned ahead the way he always did. Bent would have liked to have walked over and struck Holt hard in his smirking face. Instead he retained his impassiveness. "His trackers aren't much use, are they? I'm here and they aren't."

"That don't mean nothing. You're still a long way from away, too." Holt stopped and shifted his feet so that his spurs rang. That was the only sound besides the wheezing breath of some rider with a head cold.

"Sutton, this is a big country. Over six thousand miles of it. Which'd you like — six thousand miles of ride-away room — or to be stuck six feet under it?"

"You offering me a trade?"

"Yep; a trade. Ride out an' never come back — or stay here and never leave."

"You're on the wrong end of the gun, Holt," Bent said softly. "I'm doing the talking here."

"No, by gosh. You hang around and you'll find it out, too."

Bent dropped his glance. He looked around at the riders, saw that they had been listening and had recovered from their initial astonishment. He wondered which ones were loyal to Holt — which to Antonia Crownover's interests. He didn't ask. His glance swept over to the two gunmen he'd bribed away from Jorry.

"You know the riders, boys. Who's for Holt and who's for the outfit?"

The taller, dirtier of the duo grinned at Holt's quick intake of breath and quicker twist of the head. He ignored the glare of the foreman and the flat look of his mouth. "I reckon on'y one's a Holt man. That 'un. Swegert. They're always whisperin' together off by themselves."

Bent turned and caught the look of sudden

fright on the rider Swegert's face. He nodded toward the man. Soapy and A. J. moved in. The younger Fowler glanced over. "You want him rapped, Kid?"

"Just tie him like a turkey, A. J. He'll carry better that way."

They went to work with two lariats. Before they'd finished the last knot, Swegert was helpless and quaking with fear. His eyes moved with the swiftness of a cornered rat. He said nothing, and Bent looked back at his two hirelings.

"You earn that other five hundred, boys?"

The temptation to lie was strong in two faces at the same time, but the answer, though reluctantly given, was truthful. "Nope. He never give us a chance. Maybe, in another day or two . . ."

"All right, you can still earn it. Tie Holt's arms behind his back; then go fetch your horses. You'll ride with us and sort of watch over him. All right?"

"Yep."

Bent moved aside and let the men go past him out into the grey morning. Amos Fowler watched them both with a dry glance, then slouched out into the chill weak light behind them. He never had gotten used to trusting men behind him, especially ones that looked like these two.

Bent waited. The silence was stifling. Holt's face had a sheen of unhealthy sweat over it, but he still made no move. Not with two men behind him and one in front. That would be suicide.

The two gunmen came back, leading hastily saddled horses — not their own but choice animals. One stayed outside while the other went past Bent with a wicked smile and stared squarely at Holt as he reached for a rope. "Turn around, Mister Foreman." He helped Holt with a rough twist.

Bent waited until it was done; then he jerked his head sideways. "Mount him on something and let's get going. Soapy — you and A. J. unload their guns." He looked at the Crownover riders. "Boys — if you aren't in this — don't get in it. It's safer that way. Tell Miss Crownover she'll need a new foreman. This one won't be back. Just one thing more, boys — don't. Whatever you're thinking right now — don't. Sit tight and give us a half-hour anyway. Adios."

Amos was standing outside so that the lamp light fell on his seamed, weathered face. His little eyes flickered now and then but never blinked. Bent went out where he was and spoke softly.

"The same trail going back, Amos. I'll give you a little start, then catch up. All right?"

"Right as rain, boy. Back to the same place?"

"No," Bent said slowly, "I don't think we'd better. What Holt said makes me wonder a little. Well, I'll catch up with you anyway. We'll decide then."

"Sure 'nuff," Amos said, and turned away.

CHAPTER SIX

When Bent caught up with the Fowlers, Amos was hanging back, waiting for him. The older man had a carbine athwart his lap. "Didn't you want that Swegert, too?"

Bent shook his head. "No, scaring him was enough."

"All right," Amos said. "Now where do we go?"

Bent frowned and looked at the lightening sky. Visibility was fair. "We'd better head south, Amos, but ask A. J. to ride on ahead and scout things ahead of us. Maybe Holt was telling the truth about Jorry having manhunters out."

Old Amos nodded his head slowly. "He wasn't lyin', boy."

Bent looked over at him quickly. "How do you know, Amos?"

"Asked him while we was waitin'. Took Soapy's quirt and asked him."

Bent kneed his horse up a little until he was in the circle of horsemen. One glance told him all he had to know. There was a livid purple stain diagonally across Van Holt's face. Amos had struck him hard. Holt's eyes were murderous and black. His mouth was all but hidden in the white, scored splotchiness of his face. Amos spoke from behind Bent, staring at Holt.

"He says Duncan's got lookouts on the peaks, Kid. Says they been there since yesterday."

Bent didn't take his glance from Holt's face. "All right, Holt — what's he plan to do?"

"Danged if I know."

Something brushed Bent's sleeve. He looked down. Amos' hand was there with the heavy quirt, offering it in silence. Bent looked up quickly and caught Holt's glance at the thing. "Once more, Holt. What's he working towards?"

"They'll watch until they see you, then track you down, surround your hideout and kill you."

Amos made a rasping grunt in his throat. "Kid, Duncan thinks you're still alone. He don't know about us bein' here."

"That right, Holt?"

"How could he?" the foreman said. "You was alone every time I seen you."

Bent turned and looked at Amos. "Then we'll go on letting him think that, Amos. Listen — take Holt here to the lava beds an' leave him at my cache there; then split up and see if you boys can get behind these trackers. Just follow 'em, boys; don't jump 'em."

"And," Amos said, "what'll you be doin'?"

"They know me, Amos. I'm going to ride along the ridges until I've got a few of them on my backtrail; then I'm going to lead them over to the meadow. I'll hole up in the rocks over there — up on that old Injun lookout point — and wait until you boys are in place behind them. Then we'll see who's got the whip hand."

"Well," Amos said doubtfully, "whyn't the rest of us just ride fer the meadow and get set for 'em? Then you lead 'em in an' we'll massacre 'em."

Bent shook his head. "I thought of that. It's simplest, Amos, but suppose they all don't come? With you boys trailing them in, one of 'em will get away. I mean — they won't be able to head back to town and fetch up men or bring down the law on us."

"Yeah," Amos said thoughtfully. "All right; we'll sort of herd 'em to the place if they look like they're going to balk. But maybe we'd best take Holt to the meadow with us. He might get lost or loose over at the lava beds."

Bent shrugged. "Take him along if you want, Amos. I just thought it'd be easier to follow the manhunters without him. He might let off a yell and spoil things."

A. J. spoke up. "Well, s'pose I was t'ride on to the meadow with him and keep him there with me? That way I'd be in a fix to he'p Bent if they get t' crowdin' him any."

Both Bent and Old Amos nodded to that. The older man looked wonderingly at Bent's hireling gunmen. "What about these two?"

Bent looked at the men. "You boys want to drift or stay? It'll more'n likely mean a fight."

Without any hesitation the spokesman for the duo threw a careless smile at Bent. "We'll stay."

Bent nodded his head. "Good."

Amos looked acidly at the two men but said

nothing until he'd looked back at Bent. "All right, Kid. We'll split up and see can't we drop around behind your trackers. All but A. J." He turned toward his youngest son. "You watch now — mind you. Rap this Holt on the head if he looks like he's goin' to make any noise or anything."

Bent lifted his reins and studied the surrounding hills. Duncan's men probably had found his solitary tracks leading south. He waved a hand at the others and rode away without looking back.

By going west and a few degrees north, he would be able to hit the most prominent peaks. That was what he did, riding with his eyes never still in their careful, searching study of the land. Where he saw scrub-oak and juniper clumps, sage and man-high growths of manzanita, he steered a course well beyond rifle shot. He knew Jorry Duncan well enough to know that payment for Bent Sutton would be death on delivery.

He kept northwest until the sun was well above the far edges of the world, and didn't stop until he was overlooking a great expanse of country to the west. He had never been that far toward the extremities of the Valverde country before. Sitting there with a cigarette dangling and his eyes slitted against the eye-straining distances, he wondered idly if this was also Crownover range. The answer was in the tiny specks of cattle far off.

The castle-crag country where the home

ranch was, behind and a little below him, lay back where he had to turn to see it at all. The picture was a revelation in itself. Ashley Crownover had chosen well. Not only was his home hidden amid the upthrust hillocks that made a perfect hideout and fortress, but it was in the only part of his range where a horse wouldn't tire quickly.

But that wasn't what stuck in Bent's mind. A man wouldn't ordinarily build in such a secret place. He wouldn't ordinarily have his own laws about trespassing like Crownover had had. He wouldn't have, that is, unless he wanted to stay hidden.

Bent smiled and punched out the cigarette on his saddlehorn. Which kind of an outlaw had he been: the "made" or the "born"? He turned away and started southward. They'd see him now because all the hogbacks he faced were higher than the rest of the land east of him. Riding with his thoughts on the Crownovers, he kept a wary vigil. The first man he saw didn't see him. Not until Bent rode directly across his line of vision and watched out of the corner of his eye for reaction. There was always the possibility that any man on Crownover range might be a Crownover rider. But that one wasn't, he knew. The man rode quickly down over a side-hill, and there was a metallic glint as he tugged out his carbine.

Bent gauged the distance and acted indifferent to the rider's whereabouts. He was well out of range. Leading the manhunter wasn't hard. Bent had to dismount and fake a cincha-tightening interlude, though, in order to watch his back-trail. The rider was there, skulking from covert to covert like an old coyote. He smiled to himself, mounted and continued on south.

It took him several hours to gather in a little clique of them, but he did it. He became uneasy when he failed to see a single man behind the manhunters. Still, the Fowlers were very good at this sort of thing and they would have more reason to stay out of sight than Duncan's crew would have.

Idly curious, Bent finally left the ridges for the side-hills and began an angling descent toward the knife-sharp, dark, mottled wastes that were the lava beds in the distance. Who were the manhunters? Not that it mattered, really, but he was curious. Possibly Jorry had more influence with Valverde's law than 'Tonia Crownover did. If so, then he was being trailed by the law — maybe even United States marshals. If not, they would be local cowboys and man-trackers. There were always plenty of those human wolves in the forgotten reaches of the frontier. Professional scalp hunters; bounty-hunters, men who killed for a living and did it legally and securely. To Bent and almost all other men it made no difference by what authority bounty-hunters worked. They were considered the worst of all pariahs; men who hunted down and killed other men for pay.

The lava outcroppings were close enough for him to make out the shadow of his personal lava-blister across the wide swale that marked the farthest extremity of the lava flow, eons gone. He reined up and dismounted for the last time. Standing on the little drop-away cliff, he squirmed around until he could see behind him. Two, three, four. There would be more, he knew. Maybe six or seven all told. Jorry wouldn't bother with expense when he wanted a man's carcass dumped in the dust before The Drover's Rest for all Valverde to see.

He had a savage, sardonic look in his eyes when he very deliberately made a cigarette. A lifetime of wariness had taught Bent Sutton much. The trailers behind him could get no closer than they already were without being seen. The ridges were wind-swept and open; there was no cover close enough for a rifleman. He sat there on his spurs, perched high above the rolling country southward, smoking and secretly teasing the manhunters, who he knew would be cursing in their hiding places.

And that persistently resentful thought came back to haunt him once more. "You don't believe in anything. . . ." He stood up quickly and broke the cigarette between his fingers. A long way off he saw a sparkling brilliance that would be the sun reflecting off something shiny like a man's buckle, or the silver on a bit's cheek-piece or maybe a nickel-plated gun. He wondered. . . . If it was a Fowler he sure was a long way back. It made him a little uneasy again. Being bait wasn't bad when the range was hopelessly far, but it wasn't good if something went wrong, either.

He mounted and eased the black horse over the broken lip of the hill and swung him a little so that his descent was easy and not direct. It was stiff going at best, and little cascades of small pebbles slid after them. Down in the swale his uneasiness grew. He had a developed instinct for shunning open places commanded by heights.

Riding at a stiff-legged trot and standing in his stirrups, he swept quickly over the little valley and to the sheltering lava bed; then he cut east again, riding slowly toward the meadow, letting his horse pick the route. His own attention was held by the lip above he'd come off.

It was a long wait. In fact, he had to rein up finally and sit in the silence of the dead land, out of sight beside a lightning-blasted spire of obsidian, before he saw the first manhunter appear. He was joined minutes later by two more riders. They sat up there in plain sight, shading their eyes with tugged-down hat brims, searching the wastes for Bent Sutton. They didn't see him because he wasn't moving. Then they swung over the drop-off and followed his slide marks down the side-hill. He watched them flatten out into the swale and ride bent over, watching his tracks. It made him smile a little. Something to the west and off to his right drew his attention. It was a movement. He turned and looked. A man on a grey horse — dappled and therefore still young — was riding across his forward route, which brought a quickening of Bent's uneasiness. It wasn't a Fowler, nor was it one of the hireling gunmen; it had to be a manhunter.

Bent watched. The rider was closer than the others, by far. Within moments, if he held to his present course, he'd pass well within carbine range of the hunted man. Bent's eyes tracked him even as he leaned forward a little and pulled out his carbine and held it across his lap. The rider wasn't looking at the ground at all. Tracks evidently meant nothing to him. Puzzled, Bent waited with his breath dammed up behind his teeth. The man's head swung constantly.

When he was into the breaks south of the swale he turned and threw a long glance at the three trackers. He was too far away for Bent to see his expression, but the angle of his head had contempt in it. This one was a real manhunter. He tracked, but he also thought ahead. Realization burst on Bent as the grey horse went plunging out of sight amid the twisted, tortured snarl of the lava beds. Jorry Duncan!

Bent's heart slammed up against his ribs with the knowledge. Jorry — who detested violence — had joined the chase. He wanted Bent Sutton badly enough to sacrifice the tenets of a long life of treachery and come out into the open to get him. Bent exhaled and felt the dampness of his palm where it held the carbine. The little edge of confidence he'd had up to now was shaken. They were very closely matched, he thought. Possibly Bent Sutton was overmatched.

He lifted his reins and went deeper into the

wastes, and all his old caution and training came to the fore now. On his left was Jorry Duncan on the grey horse; on his right and to his rear were the three manhunters. There would be others, he was certain.

Riding toward the meadow wasn't as simple as he had thought it would be. With men following him, it would have been simple; but with one man forging ahead somewhere to his left, he might be confronted at any moment by a gun barrel. He longed to leave the horse long enough to ascend a vantage point, but didn't dare. Not with the trailers closing in from the rear. His peril mounted as he rode. He knew it, too, but there was no alternative. Wasting no thought on what he should have anticipated, he shoved the carbine back into the boot and continued westward with his right hand resting lightly on his hand gun.

The tantalizing tip of the meadow showed abruptly ahead of him. He rode over against a rock wall below the rise of the point where A. J. Fowler was to be, with Van Holt, and uneasiness rode with him. He went farther, until the wall of rock turned and he had the entire vista of the meadow before him, and there he reined up. The silence was engulfing. The land lay serene.

He sat there listening; there was no sound beyond the steady, dull drumroll of his heart. He looked at his horse's ears and had an ingrained reluctance to dismount. The black horse had always been and still was safety. The sprawling miles of the land were safety too, but not to a man afoot. The country was his enemy as soon as he dismounted, and he knew it, but there was no other way now.

He swung down with a granite set to his jaw, unsaddled, unbridled, and hobbled the animal, took his carbine and walked swiftly toward the weatherworn and cracked little rail that led to the spot where A. J. was.

He climbed gradually, careful of his footing, and was bending low with a twisting movement to squeeze around a stubbornly growing clump of bitter-brush, with its clawing, wiry shoots, when the smashing explosion of a carbine far south and west of him, across the meadow amid a jumble of brown-grey rocks, made him fall forward face down on the narrow trail. A large chip of sharp rock fell behind him. He rolled part way over and looked up. A clean, whitish score showed overhead where the big slug had struck. Alarmed, Bent pushed himself back behind the only shelter around — the brush — and waited. The seconds ticked by. He cursed in a grating way and craned his neck to look ahead. There was no other shelter. The miserly old trail spun its way upward to the crest against the sheer face of the hill.

The sun was hot but he hadn't noticed it before. Now he did, when the sweat came out under his hat band and made his forehead feel greasy. He couldn't stay where he was and he was afraid to try and run up the little trail. Cursing with steady invective, he hunted for a tell-tale cloud of black powdersmoke. There was none. The bushwhacker knew all the tricks, such as fanning with his hat to break up the sign of where he lay. Bent looked back at the bullet mark again and guessed how high the man had overshot him. There was small encouragement in that, though, for the ambusher would have noted — and corrected — his range. He had a trapped feeling for the first time in his life. With a final oath he got to his feet, studied the trail ahead, then broke and ran for it.

The ground wasn't conducive to fast flight. It was a very old trail, little traveled except by small game. There were breaks and erosion gulches, fallen rocks and bad footing all the way. He wanted to watch the rocks where the gunman lay but couldn't. A misstep could be just as fatal as a pause. He was climbing higher above the meadow all the time.

The second shot boomed unexpectedly near and the dirt flew up five feet ahead of him. With a start, he flung up his head, then dropped it and plunged on. The next shot came from across the meadow, and almost before its echo had died away there was a savage reply from overhead where A. J. was. Bent breathed a word of thanks for A. J.'s intervention. Then, as he leapt across two gullies in his path and panted upward toward the ledge that lay not too far above, he guessed that A. J.'s shot had temporarily confused the ambusher.

The three trackers had undoubtedly found his horse and saddle by now, too. Just as undoubtedly, they were fanned out somewhere down in the meadow where one of them had seen him and fired.

When the rampart came level with his head he surged forward for the last six feet or so and flung himself flat on the ground to avoid being skylined. There he lay with his glance raking the rocks that had been the ancient Indian lookout, searching for A. J. When he saw him, it was only a glimpse of movement behind a newly erected defensive work of flat stones. Van Holt wasn't in sight. He raised his voice as he rolled away from the edge of knoll.

"A. J.? You all right? Holt still with you?"

The boy's voice came back thin and hard. "All right, Kid. Yeah; Holt's lyin' heah like he's tryin' t' dig a hole with his nose. Come on ovah."

Bent didn't move right away though. His lungs were afire from the running climb. "Can you see 'em, A. J.?"

"Saw one. Yonder — north end of the valley. He come on horseback but he shuah clumb off fast. I missed him, though."

"Can you see Amos and the rest of 'em from there?"

"Cain't see nary a thing, Kid. Wouldn't be able t' see Amos an' Soapy anyway. They're too smaht to show now."

Bent got to his knees slowly, his head low and rolling from side to side the way a bear's head rolls when he's angry. He could see the rocks across the meadow, over by the little creek, but no movement anywhere. He backed on all fours until he was hidden from view of the men below, then stood up in a crouch and loped over where A. J. was and dropped flat again. The youth turned and looked at him. The long scar on his cheek was red against the copper-bronze of his face and his eyes glinted metallically.

"You fetch 'em to the valley, Kid?"

"Three followed me in. There's another one somewhere across the meadow. I don't know for sure...." He tried to identify the last one who'd been in place ahead of him and had fired over him into the stone face of the lookout point. Then he turned and looked at Van Holt. The black eyes were studying him with a fixed look.

"Sutton." The way Holt said it was like swearing. "Sutton nothing. I know who you are."

Bent gave a brittle smile. "Well, save it, Holt. You can take it to Boot Hill with you."

The quirt lash was swollen and puffy-looking, but the black eyes were as ruthless as they'd always been. "Think you're going to outsmart Jorry, don't you? I'd like to make a bet with you."

"Be like taking money from a kid," Bent said.

"Or like gettin' the reward money that's on your head, wouldn't it?"

A. J. turned with a vicious curse. "Shut youah mouth, whiskers, or I'll ram a gunbarrel down it an' fix you so you weah your teeth on the outside of youah mouth."

Holt read the promise in the younger man's glance and subsided, but his eyes rarely left Bent's back. He was lying prone, as A. J. and Bent were, but with his hands tied he couldn't support his head. He finally laid it down on his right cheek and kept his vigil like that.

Bent cocked his carbine and shoved it forward. A. J. looked over at him and gave a dour shake of his head. "They don't show themselves, darn 'em."

"They will," Bent said. "They figured I was alone. Now they're wondering who's up here with me."

"Wish they'd come up an' find out," A. J. growled.

"They'll do that, too. Just give 'em some time."

The silence was charged with deadliness. From their vantage point the two hold-outs beheld a panoramic spectacle. Far beyond their perch was a lazy sheen of silver, a river. It was wide and irregular, as though in its progress toward a distant sea, it meandered where it willed, unmindful of a rendezvous thousands of miles southward. Bent could get an idea of the Valverde country from lying there fitting in the pieces and working them into a huge map within his head. There was far too much of it for any one man to see — even if there had been a way to see it all together, as on a map.

When a wisp of movement off to their left showed, Bent spotted it instantly and nudged A. J.

"Man over there."

"Where?"

"Over in that rock pile south of the sandstone spire with the wind-cuts in it."

A. J.'s head swung gently so that his eyes, held still, could concentrate on all the places his head moved past. But he saw nothing. "Dump a shot in theah. I don't see nothing."

Bent hunched over his carbine and made a wry face. "Too far, A. J., but I'll let him know we're still around." He lifted for elevation before he fired. The sound went splashing out over the meadow with weakening echoes. A man's voice suddenly came loudly into the wake of Bent's shot. It was hard to place right away.

"Hey! Sutton! Come down off'n there. We'll starve you out."

Bent frowned, trying to place the voice. He couldn't. "Why don't you come up and get me?" he called back.

"Don't have to," the man shouted back. "How's your water holding out?"

"Fine," Bent hollered back. "It'll last as long as I'll need it."

"Who's up there with you?"

Bent turned and looked at A. J. Beyond the younger man, Van Holt's stare of hatred shone with a dark intensity. Bent's sardonic glance went to the Crownover foreman; then he turned his head and called out once more: "Van Holt, my old pardner."

There was a long silence, then another cry from another voice in a different place. "You're a liar. We know how many of 'em rode to

Crownover's an' took Van away. You got him a prisoner."

Bent forced a rasping laugh. "Made it look good, didn't we? If you don't think he's part of my crew, step out where he can get a shot at you."

Bent turned and looked at Holt. The foreman's neck muscles were corded and his face was flooded with dark blood. He was staring into the cocked muzzle of A. J. Fowler's hand gun. Amusement was clearly visible in A. J.'s twisted look. "Go ahead," he said softly. "Call out'n tell 'em he's a liah — why don't you? Jus' make a little squeak o' any kind — Whiskers. Go ahead."

Holt didn't, naturally. His look was murderous, though.

"Sutton? Who're those other fellers? The ones you rode into Crownover's with?"

"Come on up and meet them," Bent called back. He had placed two of the manhunters. One was directly below him, probably flattened against the face of the rocky upthrust where he was safe enough, just as he was harmless. Bent dared not edge over far enough to fire down at the man, and the manhunter couldn't fire any way but straight up. The other man was north of the peak, somewhere near where Bent's horse was. A quick intuition brought him to his feet in a swirling rush. He caught a glimpse of A. J.'s startled look as he swung and ran across the point to the other side.

He'd been right. There was a movement down

there in the lava talus where boulders lay like giant marbles along the declivity. Bent squatted and waited. In time the man moved again and when he did the watching gunman squeezed off a carbine shot. The man's cry was more of a scream than a roar. It arose to quavering heights and broke, only to rise again and hold to the high notes until Bent's hair stood out along the nape of his neck and he lay prone. The wound must not have been fatal, but it was obviously painful.

The rock-slide section of the knoll got quiet after the man's last echoes had died away. If there were others down there, Bent never saw their movements. He made a cigarette and waited. Once, A. J. called over to him.

"Flankin' us, huh?"

"Yeah."

"You shuah plugged the squeal out'n thet one, Kid."

Bent smoked and watched. The slope was as still as it must have been for the last million years. He raised his voice finally. "Listen down there. Better fetch that man out of there. He's bad hit."

For a while there was no answer; then a carbine came mincingly over the top of a boulder with a man's hat on the barrel end. "Got your word — no shootin'?"

"Yeah."

The man stood up carefully, squinting up at the ledge, saw Bent wave his hand and threw back a begrudging acknowledgement. The man used his carbine as a staff as he made his way over the slippery rock to where the wounded man was. Bent saw him lean over; then the sound of his cursing came faintly through the warm sunshine.

The rescuer had to lower the unconscious man four times before he got down to solid footing again. The man who had been hit was big — a lot of dead weight. Once, the rescuer threw Bent a savage look and the watcher could see his lips moving, but no sound came back. He smoked until the staggering man was out of sight, then went back over where A. J. was.

"First blood, A. J."

"Yeah. How long y' reckon it'll take Soapy and the Old Man to work up around 'em?"

Bent went flat, shot a glance at Holt, then smashed out his cigarette. "Hard to say. We haven't been here long enough for them to work all the way around 'em. Besides, these scalp-hunters are scattered. There's one just under us at the foot of the cliff. It'll take a little time, I reckon."

A. J. looked broodingly over the north country. "I don't mind bein' th' bait," he said, "but I don't care about waitin'."

Bent swung his head back toward the meadow below — and caught sight of movement far north of him, across the swale and halfway down the distant hill. Riders. He stiffened and spoke without turning his head. "More company, A. J.; five of 'em. Yonder — coming down that slide."

A. J. cursed in surprise. "Wouldn't be the Old Man, Soapy an' them boys o' youahs — would it?"

Bent didn't answer right away. The riders were too far away. He kept his vigil until the horses had slid and pawed their way down to the shallow little meadow; then he shook his head. "Nope. There's not a sorrel horse among them. Amos was riding a sorrel."

"Yeah," A. J. affirmed. "The law then," he said distastefully.

Bent said nothing. The lead rider was a little familiar, somehow. He kicked out his horse and went racing out ahead of the other four horsemen toward the meadow. He was angling so as to miss the tip of the lava beds, too, as if he knew exactly where he was going.

"Whoever they are — they've heard our shooting or something. Know right where they're going."

A. J. raised himself up at some risk and squinted down at the oncoming men. "Well," he said softly, "if it's the law, I hope Soapy an' the Old Man don't jump up naow an' show theirselves. Be a fine fix then, wouldn't it?"

"Yeah," Bent said, screwing up his forehead and trying to make out the riders. "They're armed for bear, A. J. Got carbines out already."

They were halfway across the swale when someone down below the lookout point in the meadow let out a warning shout that rang like a bullet hitting iron, bouncing off the cliff face.

"Eb! Behind you!"

Bent looked swiftly and saw the quick jump of a man he thought he recognized; then guns went off and shouting began again. A dull-booming rifle — not a carbine this time — broke over the lesser sounds, and the roars of the man below the cliff were chopped off in mid-breath. Bent grunted.

"That'll take care of old noisy. A. J., did you recognize the feller who jumped down off the bluff behind that boulder?"

"Didn't see him," the youth said quickly, craning his neck for another look.

"Looked like Soapy to me."

A. J. swore feelingly. "I hope it was."

And it was, but by then Bent was reflecting the youth's earlier sentiments. The Fowlers wouldn't have any way of knowing about those other horsemen coming across the swale toward them. He gritted his teeth and looked worried. An exultant shout kept him from saying anything to his companion.

Four men were walking out of the rocks with four more men behind them. Bent leaped up recklessly, flinging a glance back at the riders. They were too close now, though. He could even hear their bits and spur chains faintly but distinctly. Without a glance at Van Holt's face, on which a mixture of wonder and triumph showed, he ran toward the little trail that went downward and heard A. J.'s grunt as the younger man got up and stood looking down at Holt for a moment. He reached down and yanked the captive to his feet and shoved a pistol barrel into his side and said, "Walk!"

As fast as he could, Bent went down the face of the cliff. Men were calling to one another. Someone even laughed. Bent didn't stop or look until he was leaping over the sprawled dead body of a man he knew was the one who had first seen the Fowlers flanking them and had shouted his warning. He stopped then and looked quickly toward the walking men. His two hirelings were smiling crookedly as they herded Duncan's manhunters toward him. On either side of them were Old Amos and Soapy. He counted in his mind. The wounded man would be close by somewhere, and that would make six, all told, counting the dead man. He heard a noise behind him and looked around. A. J. was trailing Holt. The foreman's face was smudged and desperate-looking. Old Amos waved casually at Bent with his gun hand.

"That's all of 'em, Kid."

Bent started forward, calling out as he went. "Quick, run 'em over here. There's more coming."

He saw disbelief and alarm flash over Amos' face. Instantly the herded men were prodded into a trot until they were gathered close before Bent. He hardly glanced at them, despite the fact that every one of them was staring at him with a fearful, curious stare.

"Where?" Amos demanded, breathing hard from his little run. "You see 'em?"

"Yeah. Five of 'em coming up the meadow

from around the lava point there."

Soapy swore and pushed the nearest unarmed man away from him before he turned and looked. Into the lapse in conversation came the unmistakable thunder of running horses. "Five! Why, it sounds like the hull darned Yankee army." He looked at his father. "We gotta move."

Bent stepped around them and motioned with one hand toward the little trail. "It isn't much — but it's all there is. Up there."

Van Holt, though, held them rooted with his words. "Too late. Look there."

They looked. The riders burst around the far angle of the meadow and reined up. Both groups had seen each other at the same time. Amos' old Sharps rifle was leaping to his shoulder when Holt tore the atmosphere with livid curses. Bent swooped in one leap and knocked Amos' gun aside.

"Hold it, Amos."

Soapy had his carbine slanting upwards for fast shooting when Bent spoke. He turned his head just enough to see what Bent meant. The others had heard Holt's profanity and understood some of it; its despair if nothing else. Bent stood stock-still beside Amos and stared at the riders. They were sitting sweat-shiny horses and making no move at all. One of them finally eased forward out of the group, and all Bent could think of saying into the thickening silence was:

"You!"

Antonia nodded. "Yes, me."

Amos looked at Bent first. Slowly his glance traveled to both his boys. There was an "I told you so" expression on his face. Neither of the Fowler boys saw it. In fact, they didn't see Amos. They saw a girl with her hair caught up in a blue bandana that darkened the green-blue of her eyes.

Bent heard her talking through the still-pounding blood in his head.

". . . told me what happened, so I sent him to see if he could find your trail while the rest of us got mounted to follow. I didn't know what you had in mind, but I didn't want you to lynch him or anything like that." She looked fleetingly at the manhunters, disarmed and as motionless as the rest of the men afoot, then back to Bent's face.

"We couldn't understand exactly what was happening for a while. A lot of men were trailing a lot more men. Some of them we recognized. They're men from around Valverde. The others, the boys told me, they thought were the men you'd had with you early this morning when you took Van away. Why? What's it all about?"

Bent very methodically put his carbine butt on the ground and sagged a little, leaning on it. "These men," he said with a gesture, "were trailing me for Jorry Duncan. These others are my friends. They were trailing Duncan's men."

"And you led them here? Ambushed them?"

Bent made a wry face. "We didn't ambush

'em. One's wounded around there in the rocks somewhere and one's dead. These are the rest . . ." He stopped, stiffening. "No — there was another one, a man on a grey horse."

One of the men with Antonia looked up. "Yeah; I seen that 'un ridin' like the devil when we come up onto the cliff over there. He must've seen us. He sure lit out."

Bent's face was a mask. "Which way?"

"Toward town, the last I seen of him."

Bent turned swiftly and started down the meadow toward where he'd left the black horse. Amos called after him.

"Wait up, Kid. What'll we do with these?" He jerked his head at the captives.

Bent looked back without stopping. Antonia's glance crossed with his. She spoke loud enough for all of them to hear. "We'll take care of them for you."

Bent didn't speak, just waved his hand and broke into a little trot. Amos looked perplexed and rubbed his leathery jaw, then looked up guilelessly at the girl.

"All right, ma'am. Where'll we deliver 'em for you?"

She smiled. It made Amos flush a little. "Get your horses and theirs. We'll take them back to the ranch."

CHAPTER SEVEN

The setting of Valverde in the great bowl of land made a not unattractive picture. Bent wasn't conscious of it except as a goal where he expected to find the fleeing Jorry Duncan. He rode recklessly; something he hadn't done since he'd reached manhood. Dust-streaked, dirty, sweaty, with a growth of scraggly beard stubble and astride a black horse that glistened with sweat in the late afternoon sunlight, he made an arresting figure as he rode down through the traffic of the town. People looked up at him in surprise. His face was like granite beneath the grime, and his hands rested easily on the saddle horn.

He stepped down before The Drover's Rest and looped the reins once, ducked under the rail and stepped up onto the plank walk. His spurs rang musically, an odd accompaniment to the hollow thumping of his boots as he crossed the planks and shouldered into the saloon. Moving among the early patrons, he went to the far point of the bar where it turned abruptly and jutted up against the wall over by the old shaggy, stuffed buffalo head. A hard, opaque glance swept over the room. Men's faces were turned toward him in frank curiosity. Under his look they dropped away quickly.

"Bran mash?"

He turned a little so he could see the bartender and the room at the same time. "No. Where's Duncan? He back yet?"

Mort had heard a lot since he'd last seen this killer, and he'd pieced together a lot more. Rumors started in The Drover's Rest. The ones that didn't always wound up there. He shrugged, noticing how tired the gunman looked.

"He might be in the office; I don't know. Haven't seen him all day."

Mort considered. Killing Ashley Crownover might not be so bad. He wouldn't hold that against the gunman. The way it was done, though, he didn't approve of. "You're taking a long chance, mister," he finally said.

Bent looked up quickly, studied the lowering, very steady glance. "Who'll recognize me besides you?"

Mort shrugged. "I don't know, but with just one life to gamble on, I wouldn't push m' luck too far."

"What've you heard?"

"You mean about Ashley Crownover?"

"I didn't kill him, but I don't expect you to believe that."

"No," Mort said honestly, and swiped at the bar without looking into Bent's face. "I've already said more'n I should have. Now I'll say one more thing. Ride, mister, while you're able to straddle a horse."

Bent shook his head back and forth very slowly. "Not yet. I want your boss first."

Mort snorted. "He's not my boss. I got a percentage in the bar is all. I don't know where you'll find him, but I know what you will find if you hang around Valverde — a shovel patting you in the face."

Bent turned on his heel and went through the little doorway that led to the card room. Duncan's office door was closed. He didn't knock or even listen. With one hand he lifted the drawbar; with the other he palmed and cocked his hand gun. When the door went inward only emptiness stared back at him. Duncan wasn't there. He didn't wait. Holstering his gun before the startled eyes of the card players, he went across the card room and out into the alleyway through the same door he'd used once before.

Long shadows were over the rubbish heaps he bypassed, following the route he'd used another time, until he came out above, and across from the livery barn. He crossed through the traffic and stalked down into the gloomy maw of the old building. The liveryman came out of his office — and stopped. Bent saw his shocked look and ignored it.

"Where's Duncan's horse?"

"It ain't here, mister."

"When'd he take it out?"

" 'Bout half hour ago. He came in and left the one he'd been ridin' an' lit out on this other 'un."

Bent's eyes brightened. "Where was he goin'?"

"God knows — I don't."

Bent took a step forward. The liveryman made

a bleating sound in his throat. "Honest, I don't know."

"Which way'd he go?"

"I know that, mister. I watched. Never seen Jorry in such a hurry afore. He fairly flew out'n town — going south."

Bent was moving his head when he spoke again. His glance was ticking off the horses he saw, looking for one with a strong heart and a big chest.

"Did he come from the direction of the saloon when he came in here?"

"No, he come over the stage road. He's been out with that posse he recruited yesterday."

"All right. You remember my black horse?"

"Yes, sir; always remember a good horse."

"He's tied up in front of The Drover's Rest. Here," Bent said, reaching in his pocket, "that'll keep him stalled and grained for a long time. You go down and get him, and bring him up here."

"Now?"

"Right now."

The liveryman went, half-walking, half-trotting. Bent went among the horses and found an ugly-headed, sour-eyed roan gelding. He led him out and looked him over. Mean, treacherous, exuding stamina and vicious durability, he was exactly what Bent wanted — a horse you couldn't ride into the ground; the kind that wouldn't quit until he dropped dead.

The liveryman came back. His face was working in terror. Bent ignored him as he flipped loose his latigo and poop strap, shoved an arm under the blanket and saddle and pushed them off. Flipping the blanket over so the dry side was down, he lashed it around the roan horse. His saddle boot hung up over the fender and he punched it into place with a curse.

The liveryman held out the bridle, and Bent thumbed it into the roan's mouth and tugged the headstall over his head. The powerful, ugly head swung viciously.

"Faster, mister," the liveryman breathed. "Hurry — f' heaven's sake."

Bent whirled with the left-hand split-rein in his fingers. "Why? What'd you see? A ghost?"

"Listen! The boys're beginnin' to figure out who you might be. They'll be a-comin' along directly. I don't want the barn shot up." He lifted a badly shaking hand and pointed toward the back door of the barn. "There. Come on; I'll open it fer you."

The panels were hardly wide enough when Bent sunk in the gut-hooks. The roan horse's ears went back and his eyes rolled with anger and pain. Like a bullet he leaped out, slamming Bent hard against the cantle. Bent had his gun palmed and cocked but he never had to use it. There were only a few men — not over half a dozen — in the crooked little alleyway. At sight of the running roan horse and the rider with the gun in his fist, they ducked.

The town fell away rapidly and the pummeling movement of the horse reached up through the seating leather to slam hard against the rider.

Where would Jorry Duncan go? There was twenty years between them, and Bent didn't know the older man's haunts any more. Off on his right he could make out the wasteland where nothing grew; the distant darkness of the lava beds. Over there were men — and a girl — but Duncan wouldn't be heading back there. He swung his head, looking for a high spot near the road that went curving eastward like an immense ribbon. There was a wooded hassock about two miles south and a little off the road. He made for it and didn't draw rein until he had to; when the roan horse was lather-sweated and breathing as if each breath were a tempest in a cyclone. Brutally, Bent made him angle up the little hill and pulled him in on the top.

The land seemed to be tilted southward; slanting toward a mythical country that perched on the brink of an unseen sea. Mexico. It was farther than five men in long relays atop vantage points could see: the desolate, broken land that stretched beyond the limits of Valverde. Bent knew it because he had lived all of his life in that fringe world of evil that festered along that unseen line where the bad from both sides congregated. He had been born down there in one of those clapboard towns, with fat blue-tailed flies and the treachery and sordidness.

Bent's eyes were sore in their sockets. When he moved them it was like dry steel grating within an orbit of glass. The glance he raked the land with was far-seeing and cold — without mercy or warmth.

The road, with its gently arcing, inward swing, was visible for more than fifty miles. In the distance, an object, little more than a speck, moved. Nothing else stirred the length of the road, and the fox-fire of a late sun, bloody and savage, painted the range with great bold strokes of red and bronze.

He rode down off the knoll and put the horse into an easy lope. Speed wasn't as important as stamina from now on. At nightfall, he slowed the beast.

The darkness came stalking with a bold stride across the flat country, dropping seeds of blackness into the gullies and throwing them profligately against the landswells where they blossomed on contact with the land and covered it with the gloom of evening.

Bent kept on. He had a knowledge Jorry Duncan didn't share with him — that flight in great, lonely places wasn't a matter of speed. He was banking on that. He knew, from atop the hassock hill, that if that distant speck was his prey, Jorry would be afoot by dawn if not before. No horse could keep up that gait long, especially one who was rarely used and spent most of his life in the cramped confines of a box stall at the livery barn.

He walked his mount for five miles, and each step was like a stab of anguish.

He held to that gait until the animal was fully recovered from his exertions; then he lifted him back into a loose-jointed lope again, and kept it up. Alternating gaits kept him awake until the night chill came down around his shoulders and worried its way under his clothing to suck away the body warmth.

Between the chill and the constant changes of gait, he had no trouble staying awake. In fact, just before dawn, the effort of locking his jaws against an inclination to let his teeth chatter set up a soft roaring in his head and he felt tired without feeling sleepy.

He stopped at a seepage spring and let the roan horse crop salt-grass and drink water. Smoking helped. At least it kept him occupied and tended to restrain the fierce urge to hurry. He sat without moving until it was light enough to see. Jorry, wily, crafty, actually brilliant, and enormously capable, would have found out by now that his horse couldn't hold up. He might have swung off the trail.

Bent finally rode on, his eyes sweeping the half-lighted world he traveled over every once in a while. But most of his attention was directed against the dusty roadway. He had no trouble picking up the hoof marks of a running horse, just as he had no trouble seeing that the toe marks dragged enough to scuff the dust. Jorry's animal was giving out — had given out by now, unless Jorry had rested it, and if he had, he wouldn't be far ahead.

The sun came out and dumped a prodigious load of new heat and light down across the land.

It was still chilly despite the light, and Bent's back and shoulders were slow to loosen up. When they did he became more drowsy than he'd been all night. To offset it, he kept his vigil over both the land and the dragging hoofprints.

Where Jorry slowed to a walk finally, the horse's prints were staggered, wandering back and forth on the road. Bent pinched up his eyes in thought, and tried to guess how many miles Duncan had run the animal and figure from that if the beast was foundered. It was a terribly long distance, but there was no way to tell unless you could hear the animal's breathing. If he got that close he wouldn't have to figure. That thought made him stand in the stirrups, but the land was dead and dazzling, with brush clumps becoming more and more frequent as he went south. He scanned every foot of it for an eminence. There was none. This was flat, storm-battered, gullied country where every mile looked the same. Only the air and scenery here were beautiful. Everything else, including the deceptive distances, was treacherous, designed to swallow up men and animals without a trace. A land of limitless silences and little water. Truly, a land where the name *"Jornada del Muerta"* (Journey of Death) had a special significance.

He stared down at the horse tracks. They were firming up; lining out in a steadier walk. Jorry's animal was "blown". He had his wind again. Bent's glance lifted and cut a cold swath down across the distance and through the sunshine that jumped up off the mica in the road dust to plague his eyes.

"He's up there somewhere, Roany. We'll get him. Just don't give out on me."

Then came a shock. Three riders were sitting on the ground a few yards off the road, smoking and watching him come toward them. By the time he saw them it was too late. He also saw the flashy chestnut horse with the flaxen mane and tail. Its flanks were tucked up and its head hung a foot off the ground. It would be Jorry's horse, ridden out and half dead.

By the way the men sat, relaxed yet alert, watching him ride toward them without moving, thin wisps of blue-grey smoke hovering over them, he guessed in an instant how it was. Renegades traveled this barren land. It was their Thieves' Highway. They couldn't make a living here, but they had safety in the vastness and they never refused an opportunity when it came along. This time Jorry had been opportunity. Two of them had good horses; the third horse would need a long rest before he'd carry his new owner very far.

"Ride over, neighbor."

The call wasn't an invitation even the way it was worded. It was an order. Bent thought fast. There was a chance he might get away if he jumped the roan horse out and fled. There was a slightly better than even chance they'd bring him down. If they didn't shoot him, at least two of them had horses fresher than his. He studied their faces as he approached. Besides, Duncan had a fresh horse now. The roan was tough but not that tough. He reined toward them, angling off the road. A stabbing glance went to their two good horses. Both were bays. One was leggy, close-coupled and fast-looking. Bent didn't give them a chance to get on the offensive with him.

"How much for that horse — that leggy bay with the Mexican saddle on him?"

One of the men laughed. It was a rippling, deep sound. He shoved off the ground lazily and his eyes twinkled. "Thousand dollars," he said with humor in his tone. "Thousand dollars cash and no 'dobe dollars, no Mexican money."

Bent wasn't just buying the fresh horse; he was buying freedom. He nodded his head and reined up. The men were looking over at him. The big man was still grinning and appraising him at the same time. Bent had them guessing. They never got the offensive. He swung off his horse on the far side. His right hand cradled his gun so that when he walked around the roan's head, they were looking into the barrel. The lazy, hard humor died out slowly.

"Dump the guns, boys." He waited, seeing anger mount in each face, then nodded at the big man. "The bay yours?"

"Yep, he's mine."

"Take that Mexican outfit off him an' lead him over here close. You keep your back to me. Turn him with you; don't get him between us or I'll kill your friends. Move!"

The big man moved. Bent watched him, dry-eyed. "How long ago'd the other feller pass by an' leave that chestnut?"

The answer came slowly, reluctantly, from a slash-mouthed younger man with eyes like a buzzard's — slightly protruding, malevolent and glassy-looking. "Few minutes afore you come along."

"What'd he say?"

"Nothin'. Just that he'd give a thousand for a fresh horse."

"How good a horse did he buy?"

"Mine," the man said. "As good as that big bay. Not as fast but tougher."

The big man turned after dumping his saddle. His eyes went over Bent's roan horse quickly, and seemed pleased that it wasn't as ridden out as Duncan's chestnut was. He led the horse close, and Bent tossed him the rein. "You do the changing."

The man glanced up at Bent's face and stalled a minute. "You stealin' this horse, mister?"

"Yeah, for a thousand dollars, I am. He's a steal at that price, isn't he?"

The outlaw looked puzzled. "Y' mean you're..."

"I mean I'll give you the thousand. Now get moving before I give you something else — something you didn't ask for."

The man turned and went to work with a hearty will. He was smiling again. Over his shoulder he threw a dry remark. "You didn't need that gun then, pardner."

"How'd I know?" Bent said. "I'm no mind-reader. Anyway, I didn't know but what Duncan'd paid you boys to hold me up a little."

The man laughed again in the same rocky way. "Well, 's'matter of fact he did, only that was in the price of the horse, y'see."

"That's why I used the gun. Not for the horse — to keep from being delayed."

"Ah," the big outlaw scoffed amiably, "we wouldn't a bothered you much anyhow."

"I reckon," Bent said sarcastically. "That other feller say where he was going — or anything?"

"Naw, just asked how far it was to the nearest greaser village below the line."

"What'd you tell him?"

"Las Cruces — it's the nearest. Maybe twenty miles from here." The big man finished his labors and held out the left rein to Bent with an unwavering glance. "He's too shook up, though. He'll never make it. Shakin' like a leaf when he stopped here."

Bent shifted his gun and dug out a roll of bills. "Here — count it out yourself."

The man did, slowly and deliberately. He handed back a much lighter wad of crumpled bills and smiled quickly into Bent's face. "Listen, pardner — for a couple hundred apiece, we'll run him down for you. What say?"

"No thanks. This is personal. Which way you boys heading?"

The big man made a vague gesture with one hand. "No place in p'ticular. Why?"

"Don't go south."

"Aw, 'course not, pardner."

None of them moved toward their guns as Bent turned the horse so it was between them and swung up. He holstered his own gun and threw them a left-handed salute. "Good hunting, boys."

They made no move toward the guns even after he kicked out the big bay and sat twisted in the saddle looking back, but their heads swung in unison, watching him go down the land like a streak.

The bay horse was fast, too. Almost as fast as his own black mount, but he could tell by the way the animal reached out for more and more air that he lacked the "bottom" — the stamina — of the roan, so he favored him a little.

The horse tracks he followed were running again. It made him pucker up his mouth and wag his head. Duncan was rattled all right. Why did he continue his headlong flight down the land if he'd bribed the outlaws to delay Bent? The answer came on the same breath the question did. Because Duncan didn't trust them any farther than Bent had.

The sun was getting downright hot. He hauled up and tried to make the bay single-foot. He didn't know how. Grumblingly, Bent eased him over into a spine-cracking trot and stood in his stirrups with his right fingers holding him upright by the horn. He rode like that until the running tracks dropped to a walk; then he put the animal into a great, hump-backed lope and held him to it. He was closing the distance rapidly now, and knew it.

Very gradually the flat country began to show patches of scrub bush that were grey and spiny-looking. The open vistas became dotted with tenacious desert growths of innumerable varieties, all of them neutral, drab colors that ran a shoddy gamut from pallid grey to mottled brown.

The road itself changed its character. The land became greyer, more thickly spread with a mat of alkali powder that sifted through the thin overcoating of dust. The powder caked on his lips and tasted sour in his mouth. It sifted into Duncan's horse's tracks, too, but not enough to do more than soften them.

Bent's eyes ached with the strain of reflected light off the unhealthy roadway, and his body was bone-weary. There was lassitude in his vigil but he drew from it a sense of bitter satisfaction. Jorry Duncan, twenty years older, much softer, less durable, would be suffering even more. His mind conjured a phantom-like image of two wraiths chasing one another over eternity. He swore aloud so suddenly the bay horse shied under him. Images, the desert and exhaustion. . . . The three things that killed a man. Three things. The number made him think of Antonia Crownover. The fifth horseman. . . . He lifted his head and glared over the distance. Before he saw the movement he said low and forcefully:

"Yes, I do. I believe in something. I'll tell you about it some day. . . . There he is!"

And it was Jorry Duncan. He was less than two miles ahead. The hot, dry, crystal-clear desert air made him look closer.

Bent closed his eyes and pinched the lids down until they watered. He rode like that for a hundred yards before he opened them and waited for the surplus water to wash away. The vision that remained was perfect enough for him to see details. Duncan was riding slowly, his horse meandering sluggishly, head down and loose-reined. Duncan was either unconscious, asleep, or close to one or the other.

The sun was lemon-yellow and two buzzards were flying high, playfully making their drifting circles on outstretched, motionless wings so that they would cross through one another's orbit of gliding flight.

Bent's face was blank with concentration and quickened interest. He roweled the bay gently. The big animal struck a left-lead gallop and held it in a sort of loose-legged, gangling way. The distance was closing. Instinctively he knew the International Line ran through here somewhere. Maybe they were both in Mexico now. He didn't care. Reaching far forward, he tugged out his carbine and levered it. The little sound was harsh in the clear air, and carried. Jorry Duncan either heard it or his sixth sense did. At any rate he jerked erect and twisted for a long look backwards. Almost instantly he sank in his spurs, and the horse jumped out in a startled way, then settled into a weary gallop.

Bent watched the animal more than the man; then he grinned. His horse, loping easily, was the fresher of the two. Jorry's brilliance didn't include fleeing expertly on horseback. That was where Bent was going to beat him. Jorry had chosen to meet Bent on his own grounds. The advantages were immediately reversed.

Riding with the hip-motion of his saddle, his upper body unmoving, Bent raised the carbine and sighted down it. Jorry's back showed wide enough but too far away in the sights. He lowered the gun and held it with both hands. The leggy bay never offered to slow down, but Jorry's horse was done. He stumbled often and careened drunkenly from one side of the road to the other. Bent threw up his head and yelled:

"Dump your guns — Duncan. Haul up and dump your guns."

The whiplash of a voice in the stillness galvanized the fleeing man. As though his exhaustion were a cape, he jettisoned it from his stooped shoulders with a smooth motion and reined off the road toward the nearest brush patch. His horse obeyed with almost its last reserve of strength. Bent reined up sharply and watched his flight. The horse under Jorry finally slowed to a walk, and all the spurring in the world couldn't do anything more than make a bloody swath. He was through.

Bent dismounted stiffly and winced. One knee

kinked under him. He had to hold onto the saddleskirt and flex the leg for a few seconds before he turned back. Jorry's horse was standing there with his sides heaving, pumping dry, hot air into tortured lungs, but the rider was gone among the brush clumps that were spaced irregularly across the bare land.

Into the silence Bent went doggedly, leading his horse as far as the nearest brush clump. There he hobbled the animal, slipped off the bridle and hung it on the saddlehorn. He loosened the cincha very deliberately before he stood off to one side, shielded by the brush, and tried to see Duncan. The silence was deafening. It seemed to press down upon a man, surround him and hold him immobile.

Carefully, Bent started forward around the brush clump, his carbine carried loose but ready. He had to pick up the tracks over by Jorry's horse, and Jorry was probably waiting for him to do just that — lying out there like a gila monster, belly-flat and beady-eyed.

Time went by in little spurts; there were moments when he was as motionless as any Indian. At other moments he moved swiftly, jerkily, edging closer, using anything he could for cover.

From the right of Jorry's horse — keeping himself behind the animal — he knelt and pulled his dust-caked hatbrim lower to aid in the study of the ground. The tracks went east a little, at least until they got around the first far brush clump; then they disappeared again. Bent swore and searched the countryside and listened. There was no sound and no movement. He swore again and licked his lips, got the alkali bitterness inside his mouth and spat twice before he stood up and moved out, always keeping the horse between him and the direction Jorry had fled.

The tracks were far apart. Jorry had been running when he went around the brush. That meant he had kept on going. Bent considered. An Indian wouldn't work it like that. He'd run so a tracker would get that impression; then he'd duck back, throw himself down and shoot the hurrying tracker through the head when he came hustling around the brush. Was Jorry that savvy? Bent doubted it. Not now — not with fear and terror squeezing his heart between twin vices. He was running in mortal fright; his past actions proved it. Bent took a risk. He walked quickly around the horse and right up to the near side of the clump of brush and peered through the spiny growth. Beyond was just more desert — more tracks and more brush clumps farther off — but no Jorry Duncan.

He went down on his hands and knees and crept around the obstacle with its wiry old limbs, and stared out over the flat landscape with sore eyeballs. Nothing; just the same running tracks. He stayed low for a long time, until he'd traced them as far as another brush clump; then he stood up and moved boldly northward, away from Jorry's tracks and toward the open spaces.

Walking swiftly, Bent held to his northern course until he figured he was as far as he'd seen Jorry's tracks go; then he cut south and hunted up a place where he could see them again. The indentations were closer together, bunched a little as though Duncan had stopped and looked back before he went on. But he wasn't running any longer, and that made Bent nod once before he turned and paralleled the tracks northeastward.

He had no idea how far he walked, twisting and turning, dropping flat and studying every place where a killer might be waiting, running down to pick up Jorry's general direction every few hundred feet, then hurrying on. Weariness was like a shadow that followed him and never quite caught up. It didn't leave him, ever, but it was in the background now.

Then he saw the tracks go down over a little swell about a pistol shot ahead, and he stopped and knelt. His eyes had a burning intensity that was altogether different from their usual cold brilliance. The tracks went over the little swell — and didn't show again on the farther side. Jorry was lying flat over there. There was no telltale movement or scrap of man to sight upon. Bent put his carbine down, butt first, and leaned on it. Very methodically he made a cigarette, lit it and exhaled. End of the trail. . . .

He smoked in absolute silence, watching the upper lip of the swell with infinite patience. It took a long time, and even then the little pushing movement wasn't anything a man could use as a target. Someone was shoving loose earth and soft alkali dust up ahead, making a fortification of sorts that wouldn't stop a carbine slug if it was six feet thick.

Bent watched without a flicker of an eyelash. It wasn't an animal doing that; it was a man. One man. He took a deep drag off the cigarette and stumped it out in the soft, fine, powdery earth, and lifted the carbine. He settled the gun athwart his upright knee and waited. There was no hurry. The little pile grew and grew as the man behind it spent his strength making a pimple on the lip of the little swale. Bent shook his head with an ironic expression. A man could be smart, even brilliant as he knew Jorry Duncan was, but only in his own sphere. Out here, in the land of the renegades — the Outlaw Empire — it was the fundamental instincts of an animal that counted. Planning ahead and fighting a secret battle didn't count. Only Apache cleverness and bullets counted.

Jorry's biggest mistake had been when he had fled on short notice into the land where the man who chased him knew every trick. Placing himself in opposition to Bent Sutton on Sutton's own ground had been fatal. So long as he had fought Bent with wiles, he had invariably won. This was different and Bent knew it. Jorry either didn't know or hadn't considered it until now.

Bent looked up at the clear azure sky. It was early afternoon. His mind approved of this.

There was no water closer than forty miles back, where he'd rested the ugly roan horse at the seepage spring. That was important. A man rode at night to avoid the hot sun and dehydration.

His heart was pumping with long, slow strokes again. His breathing was back to normal. That meant his gunhand was ready. He threw back his head. . . .

CHAPTER EIGHT

"Duncan!"

The desert picked it up and threw it from brush clump to the ground and back again, bouncing it like an invisible ball until it rolled off into the distance and was lost.

"Duncan — you fool — come out of there."

That time the echo was longer, more garbled and unmusical and lasting, making repetitions that ran into one another until they, too, had hurried off into eternity chasing themselves.

What came next was a vicious, slamming explosion that also had an echo, but a devastating one.

Bent was surprised. He had been watching the sand pile and had seen nothing. He was tempted to fire into it, but a sixth sense kept him motionless. Where Duncan had fired from — where the bullet had gone — were mysteries. He frowned. Duncan was smart, very smart. Bent had a hunch that sand pile had been purposely erected because Jorry had known Bent would see it — would know it was man-made and watch it. If so, Duncan's guile hadn't deserted him.

Bent ranged his glance along the length of the little gully. He saw nothing. It was puzzling. "Duncan! Come out of there! This is the last chance you'll get!"

"You don't have me yet, Sutton."

At least it was an answer, even if Bent couldn't place it. "But I will, man," he called back. "I've got every advantage — you've got none."

"And if I came out — what then?"

"You'll go back with me."

There was a little pause. "You're a fool, Sutton. They'd hang you in a minute back in Valverde."

"I doubt it; what for?"

"For? For the killing of Ashley Crownover, you fool."

Bent snorted. "You know I didn't kill him!"

"What I know would only hang you higher, Sutton."

"You're a smart man, Duncan. You always were. Even over in Butte City you were smart — but you're forgetting something. The killer is alive and in the hands of some boys who'll wring the truth out of him."

Jorry Duncan's answer came back in two bursts, each with a different meaning. "I know that. Why do you think I trailed around looking for you with that posse? To kill you? That wasn't important, Sutton. The men I hired would've done that. I wanted a shot at Holt." There was a little pause; then: "What d'you know about Butte City?"

Bent's answer was impersonal and drawling. "Heck of a time to ask — isn't it? You want to take it to Boot Hill with you? All right — I'll tell you. You were quite a buck there some years back, Duncan, only your name was Brittan then. That satisfy you?"

"No. When did I know you?"

Bent didn't answer. He'd placed the voice. It was at the far north end of the swale where a long stretch of open country ran like a corridor straight as a string and twenty feet wide. He lifted his carbine and fired. The explosion was deafening. A sudden flash of movement made dust curl near where his slug hit. Duncan's voice, shades higher, came into the aftermath with terrible profanity. Bent listened, then laughed.

"Like a fish in a rain barrel, Duncan."

Silence settled between them. Duncan had learned Bent Sutton was doubly dangerous out here. Finally he called out again, and his voice was normal. "Listen — if you're from Butte City you know me. All right, we've locked horns and it's over. I'll lose more'n you will. Besides that, you robbed me in Valverde, Sutton. All right; I'll give you as much as you got before, just for getting on your horse and riding off."

"Keep it. I don't want any more of your money. All I wanted was enough to finance beating you at your own game of trying to freeze out 'Tonia Crownover. It worked, Duncan. Those two riders you imported to run off her cattle — I bribed them away from you with your own money. I bought a horse from those three owlhoots back up the desert with your money. I've still got some loose ends to catch up with — using more of your money."

Duncan's voice was thick with anger. He swore at Bent Sutton, without repeating himself, for fully three minutes, then lapsed into silence again for a while. Bent's laughter was taunting and meant to be.

"Duncan — by now Holt'll be in the hands of the law. He'll have talked all right. They'll be after you like wolves directly. How's the boot feel on the other foot?"

"Holt won't talk no matter what you do to him."

"The devil he won't. How d'you reckon I found out about your trackers? Holt told me. He told me everything I wanted to know, and all it took was one lash across the face with a loaded quirt."

"Damn your rotten soul, Sutton! What's your interest in this?"

"You — that's all. Just you."

"Why? What'd I do? Why, you blundered doing a killing, and I let you keep the money and ride off."

"Sure you did. I was the best excuse you had for fixin' the blame, wasn't I?"

"Sutton, that's your business. You don't care about the law bein' after you."

"That's right," Bent said, "I don't. It's the way you worked that trick I don't like. It's the same way you got two fellers hunted down and strung up over at Butte City twelve or fifteen years ago."

"I ought to know you," Duncan said, "but I don't. All right — have it your way. It didn't work with you — so you're still free — but don't think you're going to get me, too, because you aren't."

Bent laughed. It was a genuinely amused

sound. "Duncan — in the first place, all I have to do is sit here and let the sun do all the work for me. No water, no food, no sleep — the desert'll do the rest. Second place — you're out of your element. That was the last mistake you're likely to make. I'll get you any time I want to. If you don't think so, just jump up and come out and meet me."

Duncan's rolling oaths were livid. Bent listened and knew the man was close to action. He lay flat and lifted his carbine, waiting. But what came wasn't a shot or a glimpse of a target — just more words.

"Sutton! I'm coming out!"

"Hold it," Bent said coldly. "You throw out your guns first."

"All right." There was an interval when the perspiration ran along Bent's ribs and made a tickling sensation. He didn't bat an eye nor flinch a muscle. "Here — that's the gun." A carbine came slowly over the lip of land. An unseen hand pushed it butt first so that the barrel was pointing toward Bent. His finger tightened around the trigger a little, and his voice was muffled by the closeness of the carbine stock at his shoulder.

"Turn that barrel, Duncan!"

An oath from within the gully, and the carbine's snout swung away.

"Now the pistol."

Duncan tossed the heavy gun out. It flashed briefly, dark blue and new-looking; then it fell without sound into the dust and lay there. Bent eased off his trigger finger a little and jutted his underlip to blow upward and dislodge a pearl of sweat that hung from the end of his nose.

Duncan spoke harshly, gratingly. "I'm coming now, Sutton. Unarmed and hands up."

"Come ahead." There was a basic sound of steely hardness in the younger man's voice. It must have made Duncan wonder, because he held back and called out again.

"Your word, Sutton? No shooting; you'll take me back to Valverde for a fair trial?"

"I told you what I'd do. Now come out of there or stay in — I don't give a darn."

Duncan's head showed fleetingly. His eyes raked the level ground and he stayed stooped over until he saw Sutton's pointed, cocked carbine; then he winced. "Aim it the other way," he said quickly.

"Darn you," Bent said in a soft, almost a whispering voice, "come out of there and quit talking."

Duncan's face was frozen. He ducked his head once and moved his body. All Bent could see was the humped over back and the rear brim of his hat. Then he came up a little, and there was a blinding flash and a terrible blast of sound. Bent's finger was tightening even as his right leg was slammed up against his left and a great, blinding gush of pain flashed like a muzzle blast inside his head.

His shot was wild and he knew it when he fired. Duncan's derringer ball had missed his upper body; had ranged downward and struck his right leg where it was spread out a little. The impact had shaken his own aim so that he dimly heard the carbine slug whistling off overhead through the distant brush.

Duncan was out of sight. Bent locked his teeth and waited a sick moment for the hand to come gropingly for the pistol and rifle that lay on the edge of the swale. It never came. He knew that what Duncan had fired with had been one of those little belly-guns; small in size, short in range, and terrible in calibre.

There was a ringing in his head. Very carefully he worked his way backward, agony spiraling up with every movement of the bleeding leg, until he was safely away from Duncan's view. Then he put down the carbine and sat up, looking at the welter of scarlet that showed below his knee. The bullet had struck him slantingly, penetrating the hide in the calf of his leg. It had torn through the muscles and been deflected from its course by the shank bone emerging just above his heel. The sense of burning pain was dulling. He ignored his peril and took out a clasp-knife, cut open his trousers and very carefully made a tourniquet out of one sleeve of his shirt and tied it as tightly as he could. The bleeding stopped but the pain stayed, in a numb way.

With a gasping effort he fought his way to his feet, using the carbine as a crutch. A long glance toward Duncan's hiding place showed him that both of the man's guns had been retrieved. He made a snarling oath and started hobbling forward. Each step was an agony that made nausea fight for release against the clamped-down, tightly corded muscles of his throat.

With a smooth movement he drew his hand gun and held it cocked in his left hand. Walking with the dragging, crippling stagger of a badly wounded man, he went toward Duncan's swale. Very gradually, the inside slope of the place became visible. Then he saw the dark, rumpled clothing of the man, and three more steps brought him close enough to see his face.

Duncan knew he had scored a hit, but he was lying bent and flattened, waiting. When Bent didn't call out, he lifted his face to shout to him — and was looking into the deadly, anguish-racked eyes of Bent Sutton standing above him with a cocked gun. Their glances held for a fraction of a second; then Jorry Duncan made a shrill, choked sound and rolled to his left, bringing up his pistol.

Bent fired. The recoil made him stagger. He thumbed back the dog and let it slide away from beneath his sweat-oily thumb and hauled it back again.

Jory got off one shot, then another. Bent's first slug had torn into his vital soft parts, making him flatten against the spongy earth. There was a sense of shock but no pain right away. Duncan drew back the hammer and fired again, but he had been hit again so that his own shot was wild. A sudden deluge of bright red filmed his vision. With it came a quick warmth; a pleasantly faint feeling. He let his head go forward. Dimly he heard a third shot and felt protesting pain; then the red became a deepening purple that darkened and became black.

Bent watched Jorry Duncan go down on the soft ground as a sleeping dog goes down under a tree in the hot shade, and die. He didn't thumb back the hammer for a fourth shot. It wasn't necessary.

The pain in his leg became more insistent but he still stood there another two minutes; then very gradually he lowered himself and went to work on his wound within sight of the dead man but without looking his way. Not until he had fashioned a bandage that would last for the long ride back did he look again. A sharp glare off something on Jorry's left made him move his head and squint his eyes. The little belly-gun, nickel-plated, with an under-and-over barrel and identical .41 calibre snouts not more than two inches long, lay in the dirt. Bent looked distastefully at the thing, then turned deliberately and used the carbine to get up again, hobbled over to the brush clump he'd used to hide from the dead man while he tended his wound, went down again, dropped the carbine, lay back and slept.

It was the cold that finally awakened him. He opened his eyes and found that he'd instinctively worried himself deeper into the sand and bunched up. Thirst was a factor, too. It ran with the fire and fever in his bloodstream. He sat up and winced from stiffness. The leg didn't hurt except when he moved it. He made a cigarette, smoked and looked up at the sky. It was very late. Somewhere northward a coyote — probably scenting blood — raised an eerie, mournful cry that was as lonely as death. He listened and liked the sound.

When the cigarette was small, he ground it out and tried to get up. The effort was far easier than he'd imagined it would be. Standing, he glanced over to where Duncan lay. Nothing was changed. He hobbled over and went down into the gully and knelt awkwardly, favoring the swollen leg. In Duncan's shirt he found seven thick bundles of money. He stuffed them inside his own shirt and searched no further, but began a very tedious, very laborious ritual of desert burial.

It took a long time to do it, but when Jorry Duncan was finally buried and his killer had piled rocks upon his grave to form a cairn that would keep out the coyotes and foxes and little spinner-wolves that inhabited the desert, it was still long before dawn.

Bent went over to the horses without glancing back. He found Jorry's mount standing drowsily beside his leggy bay and loosened the animal's cincha a little before he looped one rein around the saddle-horn and put the other across the neck of his own horse and tried to mount by using only his left leg. It wasn't easy, but he had no choice. The right leg had to be helped by hand around the cantle while his left leg remained stiff in the stirrup. As soon as he worked the leg down the horse's side the pain started. He made no pretense of feeling for the stirrup; the leg was too badly swollen.

He reined the bay horse over the desert toward the lonely grave with its oddly arranged cairn of rocks. Then he reined up and looked down at the mound. From a horse's back the thing looked a lot more impressive. The words spelled out the names evenly, and the sheen of the moonlight washed them with a contour-softening mellowness:

Here Lies The Father Of
The Verde River Kid
★ ★

May God Have Mercy On
His Soul
His Son Didn't
★ ★ ★

It looked as he had imagined it would while he was creating it in a haze of pain. From up on the horse's back, with the soft moonlight washing down upon it, it had the desolate loneliness of all desert graves; lost in an immensity of country so vast no one might ever find it again before windstorms covered the cairn. Maybe a sage shoot would grow upon it, deriving nourishment from a hidden, secret source no man would ever suspect.

Pulling his horse around, he struck out at an angle for the road, to the north. Every shuffling step of his horse caused a pin-prick of pain. He felt tiredness in the muscles that ached dully and persistently. The sleep had helped little. Thirst, and to a lesser degree, hunger, bothered him, but foremost was the injured leg with its nagging insistence on rest and attention.

He rode steadily, Jorry Duncan's horse trailing in a listless way but without pulling on the rein he'd looped, lariat-wise, around the saddlehorn. He rode with the north star as his companion until it began to flicker a warning that daylight wasn't far off. A pulsing fever in him was like a cadence of slowly beating hearts, even after the sun came up.

The land looked the same. It never changed and never would, but the man and the horses had changed definitely just through associating with it. They kept plodding along all day without a stop, through the heat. Bent caught himself responding to two mirages; one in the morning, the other just after noon. He saw the third one, riders in the far, far distance, but by then knew enough to attach no significance to what he saw.

By the time long shadows were swirling around him, his tongue was thickening and thirst was like a dry flame. He held himself in tightly and concentrated on landmarks until he knew how far ahead the seepage spring was, and tried to think of only one thing — water.

It wasn't always possible, though, as the hours went by with leaden steps. His mind wandered twice, badly. Once, when he remembered the Crownover girl. When he abandoned the thought of her, Jorry Duncan's face rode through the early twilight just ahead of him. He nodded his head very solemnly at it.

"Duncan — Brittan — I don't know. I'll never know. I don't really care, I reckon, Duncan — except that a man should have a name. You know that. I was going to tell you — but it didn't work out that way. It don't make any difference, though, does it? Maybe better this way. It wouldn't have kept you from wanting to kill me — or me from wanting to kill you. Want to know how I knew, Duncan? Sure — I'll tell you. I went back to Butte City one time — heaven knows why. My mother was still there. Old, though, Duncan, and burnt out from liquor. Had fits when she'd see things and talk to them. She didn't know I was a real person when I went into the shack. She told me then, Duncan. Her name? Man — you ought to know it. Both of you had a lot of them; just me that don't know which one's the right one. Mamie Summers, Duncan. . . ."

The horse trailing behind nickered anxiously. It jarred Bent out of himself. He closed his eyes tightly, then opened them. There was nothing to see, but he knew what it was as soon as the bay quickened his steps. Water. The seepage spring.

He climbed down while the horses were drinking. It was sheer torture. He hobbled around where the horses wouldn't step on him, lay flat, thumbed his hat far back and put his face down. The stuff smelt of sulphur and rotten eggs — but it was wet! Drinking was good, but just lying there and letting the cool ground drain away the fever was better. He drank and slept without knowing it and awakened to drink again. There was a shaft of blue-grey, like the belly of a dead fish, off in the east. He looked at it without quite believing, staring with eyes that were swollen and tired. Dawn! It couldn't be. He'd only just gotten to the spring. Well, it was. That or the end of the world, because the east didn't lighten unless it was dawn.

He rolled back over and lay on his side. His hat was off and the dull sheen of his hair was bronze where it had been tamped down with sweat.

The sky looked good — far away and good. The stars were tiny spur rowels that blinked as riders rode by him. He could hear the sounds even — spur rowels and rein chains and —

"Horses over here, Ev. Two of 'em."

That wasn't a rider in the sky; that was a voice on the road within pistol distance of the spring. All of his old wolf instincts came back in a rush. He was sitting up without being aware of having moved at all, and his fist was curled around the butt of his gun. Too late, he remembered that he hadn't reloaded it. With a ragged curse he got up and almost groaned. The injured leg wouldn't even hold him. He had to hop around and snatch out the carbine. A horse nickered in the grey night somewhere, and with a sinking heart, he saw several shadows coming toward him.

"Yeah, I see 'em now. Ain't black though. Hey, Fowler? You see 'em?"

"Shuah. Better go up a-whistlin'. Folks sometimes shoot firs' in the dahk."

Bent's breath went out of him in a long sigh. He lowered the carbine and used it to lean upon. "A. J.? That you?"

"That you, Kid?"

"Yeah."

"Long way from home, ain't you?" The drawl came back.

Bent waited until he could line them up on the horizon and count them. Five, six, seven — eight. "Who's with you, A. J.?"

The first riders reined up sharply at the brusqueness of Bent's call. They sat like statues until another rider rode past them in a flat-footed walk and kept right on coming. Bent watched that one rider uneasily. When the man swung down he caught sight of a shadowy smile.

"Amos!"

"Sure as you're a foot high."

After that they all got down and clustered up close. Amos and Soapy whistled when they saw him, and A. J. let out a thoughtless cuss word. Something metallic flashed in the sickly light on one of the other men's shirts. Bent stiffened. Amos saw it or felt it, and wagged his head back and forth.

"Nothin' t'worry about, Kid."

Bent ignored him. "Who's that back there? Those other fellers. . . ."

Amos was close enough to look over into Bent's face and see the high splotches of color and the sunken cheeks. "That's a posse from

Valverde. Now listen, Kid, you got n'call to worry."

"No?"

"Naw," Amos said, half turning. "Where's that danged buggy, boys? This man's in no shape to ride back."

"Right here."

Bent recognized that voice too. His mind flung away from it angrily. "Amos — I'm not going back."

"Th' heck ye're not," Amos said in pure astonishment. "Why? You are in no fit shape to go lopin' around the danged country now." He looked worried and turned away again with irritation in his face. "Fetch that buggy up here, will you please — ma'am?"

It came, a tangle of movement in the skein of the night. Bent looked impatiently past the team to the driver. She was sitting up there on the spring-seat with the blue bandana holding in the wealth of her hair and her hat pulled forward so that it shadowed the lower part of her face.

Bent made as though to turn away. The word was wrenched out of him. "No!"

Amos looked real worried. He didn't say anything; just looked up into Bent's face, his small eyes steeped in perplexity and confusion. A big man moved around him and stood in front of Bent. The whitish glint on his shirt front was a circlet of metal with a star in the center of it.

"Listen — Mister Sutton — you're shot up. You'd

better let us haul you back to Valverde to a doc."

"Who're you?"

"Deputy United States marshal out of Raton. Name's MacLambach."

Bent's face was closed against the world. Only the fever brightness of his eyes showed through the impassiveness. "Let you haul me to hell!" he said viciously.

The marshal was as stumped as Amos was. He stood there owl-eyed, unmoving and not knowing what to say or do. Bent Sutton's reputation with his gun — and the look he had right then — were enough to stop any sane man.

But it wasn't a man who pushed in between them and planted herself in front of Bent, close enough so that all she had to do was lean a little to touch him. Her eyes were large and round and bluish-green, but he didn't notice.

"Bent — please. That's why we brought the buggy, in case you were hurt."

He blinked down at her. There was perspiration beading his upper lip and forehead. "Well — I'm not hurt so's I can't travel. Got a lot of places to go yet."

"You haven't," she said swiftly. "You haven't a place left to go or a thing left to do. Van Holt signed a confession. The marshal here has it."

The marshal was watching his face over 'Tonia's shoulder. Bent saw it and looked across at him. "D'you want me, Marshal — for anything?"

There was a little hesitation before the answer

came back. "No, Mister Sutton — why should I?"

Antonia reached over very gently and took his hand, held it between both of hers and pressed hard. "Get in the buggy. I want to talk to you."

He looked down at her again and said a ridiculous thing. "I've got two horses — y'can't just leave your horses standin' by a water-hole on the desert, y'know."

As though vastly relieved, the other men looked at one another, and Amos lifted one hand and let it fall. "We come with lead ropes, boy. Nothin' to it. Nothin' to it at all." He turned to his two sons, who were looking at Bent with worried glances. "Shuffle yourselves, lads. Lead Bent's horses whilst he rides in the rig."

'Tonia pulled his hand toward her and turned, leading him. The marshal moved to help, but Bent shook his head. "Nothin' to it," he said scratchily, "nothin' to it at all."

They started back, and for the first few miles he sat there looking at the napkin-wrapped bundle 'Tonia had put in his lap, or looked as if he were staring at it. But he wasn't, she found out when she leaned far over and looked up into his face. He was sound asleep. She let the horsemen drift on ahead. All but two; Amos and the marshal had taken advantage of the new dawn light to back-track.

When he awoke his leg was throbbing with every beat of his heart, but his head was perfectly clear. He looked around at her in mild surprise.

"Where'd you come from?"

She didn't answer the question. "Eat. You've been balancing that bundle in your lap for the last ten miles."

He looked blankly at the package, then began very gravely to unwrap it. "Food." He took up a stiff piece of cold beef and bit into it. "Food," he said again. After that he ate it all and left no scraps and mopped at his cracked lips with the napkin and dozed off again. She drove in perfect silence, waving at the riders who turned and looked back every once in a while.

Bent awoke again in the late afternoon and watched the Valverde country ahead. He sighed and made a cigarette and smoked it with a speculative glance at the girl beside him. "All right," he finally said, "tell me about it."

"About what?"

He waved the cigarette-bearing hand toward the horsemen ahead. "Them, for one thing. Who are they? And you — where'd you come from?"

"Oh." She told him patiently how they'd found him — all of it — then turned and looked straight into his eyes. "The United States marshal from Raton said — well — that there was no way for them to extradite you from Arizona Territory to New Mexico Territory — unless you'd sign a waiver or go back over there again."

"That so?" Bent's head lowered. He looked at the freshly bandaged leg. "You do that?" She nodded. "Why?"

"Do you have to have a reason for helping people?"

"I do," he said.

"No — I don't believe that, Bent. I don't believe that at all. You didn't have a reason to help me." She could have bitten her tongue off as soon as she said it. She reached over quickly and put her hand on the back of his. "I'm terribly sorry — I didn't think when I said that."

Very slowly he lifted his glance and looked at her. "What do you mean?"

"Well — about what happened back there."

"What do you know about it?"

She shot him a quick look from under her lashes. "Nothing, only that you were alone when we found you."

"Oh. Well — forget it. I'm going to."

"One question — then I will. Did you kill him?"

"Yes!"

They drove on until he heard men riding behind them and twisted to look back. The Federal marshal and Old Amos were coming at a loose gallop. He frowned. "Where've they been?"

She heard the antagonism and anxiety in his voice. "Making sure," she said. "That's all."

He faced forward and looked at his hands, opening and closing them several times, and said nothing. She waited until the two men had swept by, avoiding Bent's face and throwing them both a slow grin and a wave, before she spoke again.

"Bent? There isn't much time left and I've got a lot to say. Do you mind?"

He shook his head without looking over at her. "No — go ahead."

"Well — once you said you'd never worked for a cow outfit. I need a new foreman. The Crownover's big. It takes men to run it. One man especially. Would you do it? Take the job, I mean?"

He kept his silence, but he was looking at her with a strange expression. She saw it and turned away, words coming to cover the confusion she felt.

"Really — it's more than just that. You need it."

He interrupted her swiftly. "The fifth horseman, 'Tonia?"

"Don't be sarcastic, Bent," she said quietly. "I know what you're thinking. That and the other things I've said to you — like on the day of my father's funeral — about not believing in anything that's good and worthwhile — maybe I shouldn't have said those things, but they're the truth. I don't know why you're that way — but you are — and you shouldn't be." She drew a wavering breath and looked him fully in the face.

"Bent — I don't want to change you; I can't. I want to see you changed, though, and I think you will change. But it'll have to be something from within — something you do yourself. Will you take the job?"

He looked up ahead. Then he turned and settled back against the seat, looking at her.

"Would you like me to tell you a story about a kid that became a top-notch gunman?"

She faced him and nodded, and he didn't see the tiny quiver of her nostrils. "I'd like that very much."

So he told her — leaving out nothing right up to the present. She was appalled and shocked — and a little thrilled too. When he finished a strained silence settled between them until he wiped his palms on the outer edges of his pants and made a harsh little laugh.

"So — 'Tonia — that's the kind of a man you're asking to be your foreman."

She looked over at him very steadily. "That's just exactly the man I want to be my foreman."

He blushed like a kid and fumbled with his cigarette sack. Ruefully he concentrated on the cigarette and avoided looking at her. "All right, ma'am. You've just hired an honest cowboy — but you'll have to teach him the cow business. Maybe more'n that — even."

Her heart lurched and she looked up with a very warm glance. "What else, Bent?"

"Well — for one thing — about those four horsemen of the something-or-other you told me about once."

She let a laugh come out with a rush. "I'll do that, too, cowboy."

Their glances crossed, and for some strange reason the electrifying shock that passed between them made them both laugh aloud together, and Old Amos turned with a worried look and squinted up his eyes in wonder, and wagged his head from side to side.